CW01022335

DATE WITH DEATH

WELCOME TO HELL #3

EVE LANGLAIS

SECOND EDITION

Copyright © June 2013, Eve Langlais

Cover Art by Dreams2Media July 2017

Produced in Canada

Published by Eve Langlais

www.EveLanglais.com

E-ISBN: 978-1-927459-39-3

Print ISBN: 978-1-988328-73-7

ALL RIGHTS RESERVED

Date With Death is a work of fiction and the characters, events and dialogue found within the story are of the author's imagination and are not to be construed as real. Any resemblance to actual events or persons, either living or deceased, is completely coincidental.

No part of this book may be reproduced or shared in any form or by any means, electronic or mechanical, including but not limited to digital copying, file sharing, audio recording, email and printing without permission in writing from the author.

"FUCK HIM!" Crumpling up the offending parchment, Lucifer tossed it in the air, and with the twitch of a finger, ignited the missive that put him in a foul mood.

Lowering her e-reader to peek at Lucifer, Gaia, his currently on-again girlfriend, said, "I didn't know you swung that way."

"I don't. I meant it figuratively, not literally."

"Ooh, big words. Has someone been brushing up on his vocabulary?"

Mouthy wench. Lucifer shot Gaia a dirty look. "Aren't you the funny one this morning."

"Funny? Me?" She batted her lashes in an attempt at innocence that failed. "I was just impressed with your oral skills."

"I prefer it when you scream about them, not mock."

"Noted. So, who do you want to fuck?"

A shudder went through him as the vulgar word

slipped past her lips. Hearing Mother Earth cuss always turned him on. "I always want to fuck you."

"Are we talking figuratively or literally this time?" She tossed him a sassy grin.

He growled, a sound that always sent his minions scurrying.

Not Gaia. She laughed. "It never hurts to ask. Last time I told you to kiss my ass, you—"

"Dropped to my knees and did it with pleasure." His girlfriend did have the most delightfully plump posterior. Lucifer leered at her, but she missed the suggestive glance having gone back to her book. Such impertinence. Only she dared treat him like a man instead of an almighty deity. "I swear he does these things to throw my game off."

"Who, dear?" Gaia absently asked as he paced the foot of an ornate, four poster bed—also known as the nest of original sin, at least according to the monthly publication, *Hell and Garden*. "And what did he dare do to rouse the renowned temper of the great and mighty lord of Hell?"

Out puffed Lucifer's chest. He never could resist a compliment. "Who else but that has-been god whose name I refuse to utter." Because the more someone believed and spoke about a deity, the stronger they became. Power came to those with worshippers. This energy boost was the main reason Lucifer enjoyed stirring up trouble on the mortal side. Nothing like keeping his name in the news, and bandied about in churches, for a magical rush. "The bastard has been taunting me with our upcoming golf match."

"Taunted you? How in the pit did he manage that

because last I heard you bellow, you weren't on speaking terms with him."

"I'm not. But my spies say he's been running his mouth."

"As have you."

"That's different."

"Of course it is." She rolled her forest green eyes. "We all know the universe revolves around you."

He chose to ignore the sarcasm in her tone to focus on the truth. Usually a dirty word, but in this case, apt. "I know it does. Which is why I've got a plan to get him back."

"Does it involve killing him, maiming him, or starting an interdimensional war?"

"No. No violence, at least on my part." Lucifer paused his pacing to ask her with a most serious mien, "Do you think this means I'm losing my touch?" Did the fact he didn't plan murder and mayhem say something about him as Lord of Sin?

Gaia put aside her electronic device and gazed at him. "Oh, I'd say your touch has never been better." She winked as she licked her lips. Instant boner. "You know I find a finely-tuned, eloquent revenge so much more satisfying than a plain old war. Sexier too. You know how I love it when you get devious." She purred the last bit.

And she was right. He did know how much Gaia enjoyed subtle revenge. The whole world did. When Lucifer rocked Gaia's world, she rocked the mortal one. Blame his incredible prowess for the plight of mankind—when the bed started knocking, the earth got a shaking.

Sucked for the humans, but here in Hell, it just served to enhance his reputation.

Booyah!

Back to his nemesis, though. Time to set the plan in motion. He had an opponent to frazzle and a golf game to win.

ONLY ONE INGREDIENT TO GO. Marigold dangled the last bit over the boiling cauldron and began reciting the words to the spell that would grant her something she'd longed for all her life. A prize without compare that modern cosmetics promised but never cured—getting rid of her bloody freckles.

Giddy with anticipation, she took a deep breath and continued her chant. "Hair of the divine beast, grant me the wish I seek." Corny, but then again, she'd not created the spell. She held the glimmering unicorn hair over the bubbling brew, a frothy concoction she didn't really want to drink because it smelled and looked icky, but drink it she would if it would help. Down drifted the glimmering strand and it sank in the potion with an ominous sizzle.

Hmm, I hope it doesn't do that when I swallow it.

Using her wooden spoon, she stirred the concoction as it bubbled and steamed. When the prescribed sixty seconds passed, Marigold opened her mouth to say the words to invoke the spell when she heard a rustle of fabric.

Whirling from her stove, and the vile brew, she noticed a cloaked figure standing at the edge of the candlelight, a scythe in one hand.

Seeing as how she'd locked her door and lived on the eighth floor, his presence didn't bode well. "Who the hell are you?" she asked. As an added precaution, she snatched her ritual dagger and brandished it in front of her.

"You can see me?" Judging by his tone, the hooded stranger seemed taken aback.

"Well, duh," she replied, rolling her eyes. "You're, like, standing right in front of me. I'm not bloody blind, you know."

"But you're not supposed to see me." Again with the incredulity. Welcome to the club. He thought she shouldn't see him, and she thought he shouldn't be there. That made them even of a sort.

"Not only can I see you, but I'd like to know just how the heck you got in here?" The doors to Marigold's apartment were not just locked, she'd spelled them as well. So how had he gotten in without setting off any of her alarms? Maybe he was a demon. Or a ghost, or...

"Death cannot be hindered by a mere mortal lock," he announced pompously with a wave of the scythe. The stranger had an accent, which despite the strange circumstance, Marigold found hot.

"Death?" Marigold giggled. "Oh, come now. You're not big or scary enough to be him." At just over six feet, or so she gauged, while wide of shoulder, her visitor lacked the ominous presence and stature she'd always imagined a true god would have.

A growl emerged from the cowl shadowing his face. "I might not be the actual Lord of Death, but I am one of his lieutenants. Now, do you mind stopping the idle chit-chatter and getting on with what you were doing? I've got other appointments to keep."

But Marigold's mother, despite her ditzy nature, hadn't raised an idiot. "Wait a second. If you're here to collect me for the underworld, then that must mean I'm about to do something deadly." She eyed her steaming cauldron and sighed. "I should have known better than to try a spell I found on the Internet."

Blowing out the candles—four black, tallowed ones, one for each point of the compass—she carefully stored the remaining unicorn hair, a precious commodity that had cost her dearly—and turned to face her uninvited guest with a smile. "Sorry. I've decided today is not a good day to die. See you in, like, oh, one hundred years."

"You've got to be fucking kidding me." Death's agent didn't sound too happy. Lifting an arm, the loose sleeve of his robe fell back and a large hand—covered in skin and not just some bony protrusion—pushed back the hood. Blazing eyes regarded her, but that wasn't what made Marigold speechless. Talk about a handsome hunk of man.

For some reason, when she'd pictured Death and his minions, she'd expected skeletal figures with spooky, coal red eyes. Reality vastly differed, in a good way. Towering over her smaller frame, the Grim Reaper's minion glared at her with intense dark eyes, chiseled features that included high cheekbones, a straight aristocratic nose, square jaw—covered in a sexy stubble—and full, sensual lips. His hair was short and a deep ebony color that glinted red in the dim lights of her apartment and set off his pale tan beautifully. *I wonder if he'd get naked so I can see if he's tanned all over?* His robe unfortunately hid the rest of him, but if his body matched the big hands and thick, muscled forearm he'd revealed, then she thought it a pity he'd taken up soul collecting instead of pole dancing as a profession.

He pointed his scythe at her. "You can't avoid an appointment with Death, so please cooperate and finish what you were doing."

Stubborn, and not one to follow orders, Marigold crossed her arms under her boobs and shook her head. "No. And you can't make me." *I think,* she added silently.

"Says who?" He took a menacing step forward.

With a bravery she didn't quite believe, but faked quite well, she dared him. "Says me. So go ahead, kill me in cold blood, you big...big meanie." As name calling went, it was quite lame, but somehow, she couldn't bring herself to call him something really nasty. Although, she wouldn't mind him doing nasty things to her body, naked, of course.

"I'm a meanie? I'll have you know women say I'm the nicest guy they've ever met."

"And is this before or after you drag their souls back to your boss?" she replied sarcastically.

"I don't mix business with pleasure."

"What a shame," said Marigold. "I guess this means

you won't be able to accept when I ask you to come back for dinner tomorrow night." The invitation popped out of her mouth before her brain could prevent it. Once extended, though, she felt no urge to take it back. The man, minion, whatever he was, redefined the term delicious. And given her current love life was at a standstill, a date of any kind was welcome, even a date with death.

"You want me to come back for dinner?" There was that incredulous tone again. "Aren't you afraid I'm going to try and take your soul?"

"Could you wait until after dessert? I make a kick ass cheesecake."

He didn't answer. Instead, still shaking his head and mumbling under his breath something which sounded suspiciously like "completely insane," he faded away. Cool trick.

Only once her kitchen gaped empty, the imposing man no longer taking up so much space, did it hit her. She'd just escaped death. Holy moly! And like an idiot, she'd invited him back. She smacked herself in the forehead.

Do I have a death wish? Although, I wouldn't mind having, what the French say, la petit mort. Also known as a big O.

As a minion of death, did that make him stiffer than a normal man? She snickered at her own corny joke. She'd probably never know. Unless she did something stupid, or if that movie *Final Destination* was based on truth, she wouldn't see him again unless she died. Bummer. She couldn't help a touch of disappointment. Who could blame her?

The man had a serious sexy vibe going on, and it had

been awhile since she'd gotten hot and sweaty with someone.

Maybe he'd come back. After all, he'd not technically replied to her invitation. Problem was, when he returned, would he do so in the role of beau or because he'd rescheduled her?

Just in case, she'd better shave.

3

MICTAIN, the Aztec god of death and collector of souls for Satan himself, translocated—a new fancy term created by the office for metaphysical terminology and scientific advancement for folding space and time to get from point A to point B immediately—back to his home in Hades. His head still shook in disbelief over his encounter with the confounding human. Not one to usually get flustered, she'd taken him off guard for several reasons. The most shocking was his immediate attraction to her. He'd lived —or not depending on how you looked at it—a long time and while he'd taken his pleasure often with females, both human and not, never had he felt such an instant desire or gotten so fucking rock hard just from a short conversation. Not that their talk was sexy. However, the witch herself? Something about her set off a chain reaction in his body.

Average of height and features, there was nothing about her that screamed drop dead gorgeous, and yet, at the same time, she drew him, even dressed in her tattered crop top and cut off athletic shorts. Was it her curly mane of brown hair that corkscrewed wildly around her face? He definitely approved of her lush frame with her wide hips, indented waist, and deep cleavage—a plump body made for pumping as his twitching cock reminded him. He even liked the way her freckles scattered across her button nose and complemented her pink mouth, a mouth he could imagine sucking him with enthusiasm. She also had pretty green eyes with dark lashes that regarded him with frank interest, which begged the question, how in the nine circles of Hell had she managed to see him?

No one ever saw Death coming. Well, they used to, but all the screaming and pleading was annoying, hence the cloaks of invisibility all the soul collectors wore nowadays. Perhaps his vestment came back defective from the cleaners? Should he test it? Easy enough to do. Off he popped to the cancer ward of a hospital he visited much too often. With a silent tread, he weaved among the beds of the sick and dying, waving his arms, shouting boo even. No one paid him any mind.

Back he translocated to Hell, more puzzled than ever. If his robe worked, then how had she pierced its magic? He'd have to file a report. Dammit. He did so abhor paperwork.

Mictain laid his scythe against the wall next to his coat rack and tugged off his work robe to hang it. He hated wearing the stupid thing. A movement started by the Grim Reaper's Union to change their mode of dress had gained momentum years back, but had never gotten anywhere. A pity because the damned neck-to-toe robes were itchy and hot. However, their invisibility feature did come in handy when worn to collect a soul, which once more made him think of the plump brunette who'd managed to see him anyway.

Itchy robe off, Mictain, dressed in jeans and a t-shirt, strode into his office and pulled up Marigold's file, wondering if he'd missed something.

Name of soon-to-be deceased: Marigold Stanton

Time and date of death: 20:38:17, February 7th, 2011

Location: Kitchen (coordinates 66:66:66:66)

Method of death: Ingestion of poisonous potion

Soul collector: Mictain

Final destination: Hell

Signed: Lucifer, High Lord of Sin

As information went, it was rather bare bones. After all, when Death came to take a person, they didn't need to know much, just when and where. Sorting them and deciding their punishment was up to Lucifer, and on rare occasions, God himself. The report unfortunately lacked some details Mictain wouldn't have minded knowing, such as her age and whether she dated anyone. That she'd merited a spot in Hell didn't surprise him. Most people had a hard time following Heaven's strict rules of admittance. Not that he cared about her nature. It wasn't like he had any interest in her other than how he would explain his failure to his boss, Satan himself.

His hellphone rang—a version of the surface cell phone powered by the souls of CEOs of phone companies. The lord of the pit had a twisted sense of humor, especially when it came to punishment. Mictain answered, recognizing the familiar number, and prepared for a reaming.

"What the fuck happened up there?" barked Lucifer, employer and longtime friend.

"You tell me. She could see me, and when she realized what I was there for soul, she stopped what she was doing." *And then she asked me back for dinner.* Mictain kept that last tidbit for himself.

"What do you mean she could see you? Nobody sees Death coming. I don't like it. We can't have people dodging their time to pass on. It was bad enough when those stupid *Final Destination* movies came out and we saw a drop in accidents. I won't stand for people seeing us and avoiding what they've got coming to them."

"What would you suggest I do then?" Mictain asked, pinching the bridge of his nose.

"We need to know more about this girl. Find out how she could see you. I need you to get close to her and encourage her to spill her secret."

Mictain frowned at his phone. "You want me to date her?"

"Date her. Fuck her. I expect you to do what it takes to make sure this doesn't happen again. She's attractive enough. It shouldn't be too hard for you to get *in*, if you know what I mean."

Mictain couldn't help thinking of her luscious curves and how they'd look even better wrapped around his naked body. However, reality intruded. "What makes you think she wants to see me again? After all, I did show up to collect her soul." Mictain didn't mention she'd asked him over for dinner; in hindsight, he was pretty sure she'd meant it as a joke.

"You're good-looking for a guy your age. Pour on the charm. Wear some tight jeans. Do something. You never used to have a problem getting women into bed with you."

That was true. Hell, he'd had multiples in bed on more than one occasion. Somehow, though, he had the feeling bedding Marigold would be different, and he didn't like even thinking that way. But orders were orders. The things he did for work. Mictain restrained a sigh. "I'll do what I can."

"You'd better. Keep me apprised of the situation." With a click, Lucifer was gone and Mictain hung up his hellphone.

Tapping his fingers on his desktop, he leaned back in his chair. Commanded to seduce a woman who enflamed his lust so he could pump her for information, along with other body parts. Subterfuge wasn't usually something that bothered him, and he couldn't deny the idea of bedding the hot witch was appealing. However, a woman scorned was bad enough; a witch scorned who could see death coming... What a cluster fuck in the making.

Despite his bad feeling about the subterfuge he'd have to engage in, Mictain couldn't help the anticipation that lightened his step as he shopped for something to wear on his date. It had been several millennia since he'd needed to charm a woman. Should he bring flowers? Chocolate? A charm to detect poison in his food? And what about a condom? While he couldn't carry disease—his deity status protected him from that—pregnancy was always a possibility, especially when fucking with humans.

Mictain reined himself in. All of this planning was well and good. None of it meant that Marigold wouldn't throw him out on his ear when he showed up in her apartment tomorrow for the dinner he'd never technically accepted.

Maybe I should wear a jock strap in case she gets violent. Which brought to mind restraints. Hmm, Marigold, spread eagle, tied to the four posters of his bed, naked and begging. He'd better get the big pack of condoms. Maybe two.

4

MARIGOLD SANG and danced as she cooked up a storm for a man—er being—who'd mysteriously vanished instead of answering her invitation to dinner. Perhaps it was optimistic of her. Perhaps it was her hormones hoping to get lucky. Maybe she just hoped she'd intrigued Death's collector like he'd captivated her. Whatever the reason, she hit the grocery store and picked up a ton of fresh food. She'd also gone to the hairdressers in an attempt to tame her wild mane, had her nails done, and, at her libido's insistence, sprung for a Brazilian wax, which was painful enough to douse her arousal for a few hours.

Of course, all this effort would end up a huge waste if he didn't show up. Her mind's attempt at a reality check didn't stop her from wearing a slinky black dress that hugged her generous curves and dipped low in the back, making a bra unusable. While not a perky A cup, her C breasts held their own, especially with a pair of masculine hands holding them. Given her lack of upper lingerie,

Marigold went for sparse lower panties. Her thong with the teensy triangle of lace in the front hid nothing, and she knew from experience it drove men wild. Marigold wondered if the hunky Reaper would react the same as a human. Just in case he went bobbing for pussy, she dabbed some vanilla scented perfume on her pubes and under her ear lobes.

Now she just had to hope he showed up and...

Warm breath tickled her nape, and Marigold whirled around with a shriek, brandishing her wooden spoon like a weapon.

Looking yummier than she remembered, the Grim Reaper's minion stood in her kitchen with a partially unbuttoned black dress shirt tucked into skin-tight blue jeans. His lips twisted into a smile of amusement, and his eyes crinkled when he said, "Wooden stakes only work on vampires."

Her pulse racing as if she'd just run a mile, Marigold put the spoon down and hoped she hadn't splashed herself with sauce when she jumped. "So glad you could make it," she said, trying to sound nonchalant. Now if only her heart would slow down.

"I thought about not coming."

"But?"

He shrugged. "It's not every day a beautiful woman asks me on a date."

Beautiful? She dared any woman not to cream her panties with that kind of compliment. As her pussy warmed up, she ogled him, still stunned he'd returned.

Up close and without the concealing robe, her dinner date was beyond sexy. Broad-shouldered, his thick arms and chest strained at the fabric covering his delicious, tanned skin. She dared not look below his waist to check out his package. She was truly afraid she'd drool, thus totally ruining her calm and collected look.

Screw it, he probably thinks I'm nuts already anyway. She peeked down and bit her lip at the bulge that stretched the fabric as she watched. *Maybe we should skip dinner and go right to dessert.*

"Would you like me to get naked so you can get a better look?" His sarcastic words, tinged with mirth, made her tear her eyes away and look at his face. His lips curved at the corners and his eyes sparked with mischief. The man just kept getting sexier and sexier.

Marigold smiled wickedly. "I'd love for you to get naked, but you might find my kitchen chairs cold on the ass seeing as how they don't have any cushions. But, it's up to you. I sure wouldn't mind some visual candy while we eat."

A giggle almost escaped her when his cheeks darkened with color. Apparently, the agent of Death wasn't used to having the tables turned on him. Which reminded her... "Do you have a name? I'm Marigold, in case you didn't know."

"I know all about you, *Marigold*." The way he said her name sent shivers down her spine and made her sex quiver. Oh, to have that mouth talking to her other set of lips. "My name is Mictain."

Marigold frowned at him. "What an awkward name. I think I'll call you Mick." With his accent and the inflection he placed on the consonants, she doubted she could say his name without mangling it.

"Awkward?" He sounded flabbergasted. "Excuse me, but my name happens to be well-known and, might I add, a worshipped one. I am the Aztec god of death."

"You mean you used to be famous. Last I heard, Aztecs were pretty much extinct. I guess that's why you started working for the Grim Reaper, huh? What with all the sacrifices having died off. Ha, died off." Marigold snickered while Mick's face went through a variety of emotions— disbelief, embarrassment, and finally, anger.

"You are the most aggravating woman I think I've ever had the displeasure of meeting."

"Flatterer. Now are you going to strip before dinner or not? Because if you aren't, then sit your sweet cheeks down so I can serve you the best pasta you ever ate."

Mick, still unfortunately clothed, and with his jaw tight, sat and Marigold spooned out two large bowls of pasta—rotini noodles covered in a white sauce with sautéed chunks of chicken, green pepper, red onion, and diced tomatoes. She also slid a platter of cheesy bread on the table, a French baguette sliced lengthwise and toasted with garlic butter then dribbled with melted cheese. *Mmmm...*

Mick picked up a fork to dig in then stopped and looked at the food dubiously. "Did you poison it?"

"Why would I do that?" she asked, taking a big mouthful and closing her eyes in pleasure as the flavor hit her taste buds. "You work for Death, so I can only assume that it might be kind of difficult to kill you. Besides, it would be a waste of good food." She took a crunchy bite of the gooey bread and groaned in bliss.

No WOMAN SHOULD EVER LOOK SO DECADENT EATING.

Mictain stared at Marigold, who sat with her eyes closed as she chewed and made happy noises. His cock hardened at the rapturous look on her face and he wondered if that was how she'd appear on her knees sucking his cock. Shocked at the direction of his thoughts, even if they sounded fun, he shoveled a forkful of pasta into his mouth and almost groaned in pleasure himself.

Damn, she can cook. As single male, and a god, food wasn't high on his list of priorities. He often ate out, or made do with quick and simple meals at home. It didn't compare to a home cooked repast.

He forwent speaking for eating, unable to stop himself from enjoying the food. The silence wasn't stilted, though, even if it was kind of noisy with the sounds of chewing and the occasional moan of bliss. Their eyes struck up a flirtatious conversation. She eyed him saucily. He regarded her boldly. She winked. He winked back.

It was the most fun he'd ever had on a date, even if this wasn't a real date, and yet not a word was spoken.

Unfortunately, the food eventually dwindled until there was just a spattering of sauce in the bottom of his bowl that he looked at longingly, wishing he had more bread.

She had a solution. She ran her finger along the bottom of her bowl and then licked it, a sensuous flick of her tongue along the length of her digit that made him harder than a rock.

He cleared his throat and opened his mouth to speak,

but lost his train of thought when she licked her succulent, pink lips.

"Cat got your tongue?" she teased.

"That was delicious," he finally managed to say.

"You're welcome."

"Do you eat like this all the time?"

"Unfortunately. Can't you tell?" She peeked down ruefully at her hips and thighs.

"Your shape is perfect." He blurted the compliment without thinking, and she shot him a startled gaze. A pleased smile curved her delectable lips.

"Thank you. I take it you don't cook?"

"Not outside the bedroom." Flirting with an ease he didn't know himself capable of, he wondered what it was about her that made him act so uncharacteristically.

Rising from her seat, Marigold cleared the table, shooing his attempts to help her. "Sit down. Relax."

Relax? With the hard-on of the century? Thankfully, he sat tucked under the table, thus hiding the evidence of his attraction. It didn't take her long to rinse the dishes and return with a fresh bottle of wine. She slid back into the seat across from him. "Now that I've fed you, I think I deserve a boon," she announced.

Mictain stiffened, and not between the legs this time. "If you are going to ask me to intervene in your death, forget it. That's not up to me."

"Oh, please. Give me a little credit. You were just doing your job. If I want to petition my demise, I'll do so with the big man himself."

"If you're not looking for an intervention then what do you want from me?" *Say my cock and I'll strip right now.*

He'd also donate his tongue, or any other body part she wanted.

"What I want is to know more about you. How old are you exactly? Where do you live? Do you have a girl-friend?" She said the last part almost shyly, running her finger around the rim of her wineglass, not daring to stare him in the eyes.

He saw no reason not to answer. "I'm not sure of my exact age. I can assure you I am much, much older than you, but never fear," he said with a grin as her gaze rose to meet his. "I've got the stamina of several twenty-year-old human males."

Despite her earlier blushes when he complimented her, this time the vixen licked her lips and regarded him hungrily. "Good to know," she purred. "Now, what about the rest of my questions?"

"I have a loft in Hell on the outskirts of the inner circle, and no, I am not currently dating anyone."

"Excellent."

"What about you?"

"I wouldn't have invited you to dinner if I was seeing anyone. I'm a one man kind of gal. Now are you ready for *dessert*?" she asked with a wink.

Mictain's cock hardened at the thought of the sweet pussy under her dress, but instead of getting naked, she held up a platter holding a cheesecake dribbled in caramel sauce. Mictain groaned.

"No more. At least not yet. I need some time to work dinner off."

Setting the cake down, Marigold grinned at him saucily. "I know the perfect exercise after a dinner like that." She came around to him and Mictain, already erect beyond belief, almost blew his load at the promise in her words. "Come with me," she said, grabbing him by the hand and tugging him behind her.

Gone was his reason for being here. Gone were the reasons why he should abstain from getting involved. All he could think of was how quickly he could get her dress up around her waist and his cock buried inside her.

She led him into the living room instead of the bedroom, which surprised him, but then again, she had a really comfy-looking couch. She wandered over to an entertainment center. Mictain dropped onto the couch and watched her, his dirty mind wandering.

I'll bet she's choosing some nice music right now, something with a sultry beat so she can strip for me and show off that curvy body of hers. I wonder if she'll touch herself in front of me. Cup those luscious breasts and...

She turned and tossed something to him as the television came on. Mictain bobbled the plastic wand and peered at it with incomprehension.

"What is this?" he asked as he watched her point her own plastic wand at the television.

"Don't tell me you've never Wii-ed?" she exclaimed. "Oh boy, are you in for some fun. There's nothing more energizing than playing a fantastic game of bowling, and from the comfort of home."

Mictain was speechless. If someone would have told him his date with a witch would end up with him playing a video game, he would have busted a rib laughing. As it was, he managed only brief answers as she spoke and taught him how to play virtual bowling of all things. Did she not see he had an erection that could double over as a battering ram, one that got worse every time she squealed and jumped up and down? Couldn't she sense the sexual tension in the air? Was he the only one fighting lustful urges? When she dropped her remote at one point she bent over, giving him a glimpse of her bare cheeks with the thong flossing them, it took all his control not to rip his zipper down and sheathe himself in her.

But, she seemed oblivious to his raging desire and much as it pained him to admit, he was enjoying himself. Marigold possessed a vibrant and playful attitude that made him smile and appreciate her for more than just her body.

She was also kicking his ass at Wii bowling. "I got a strike," she crowed.

"And I've got a bat," he mumbled.

Bright eyes regarded him with mischief. "So you prefer to hit balls, do you?"

"Actually, I'm more of a pocket poker," he said, trying to regain the upper hand with an obvious innuendo.

She took it in stride, though, and raised the bar. "I love pokers, especially when they get my hole in one." She giggled. "That has to be the worst dirty talk ever."

Mick grinned back. She was right, that truly was awful innuendo. "I'm better at dirty actions than talk."

"So am I," she said, dropping her video game remote and walking toward him with lustful intent in her eye.

Oh yeah, here's comes dessert.

"What do you say we engage in a different kind of sport?" she asked him huskily.

"Something more hands-on?" he asked hopefully.

"Hands. Body. Clothing optional. Stop me if you think I'm going too quick."

Um, would she think him a pig if he asked her to go faster?

She pushed him back onto the couch and straddled his waist, the skirt of her dress riding up around her thighs. Even through the fabric of his jeans, the heat of her core pulsed against him. Her hands gripped his shoulders and slid down his arms, squeezing his biceps. She stared him in the eye, her lips curved in a sensuous smile. There was nothing coy about Marigold. She was all woman and unafraid to go after what she wanted. Lucky for Mictain, she wanted him.

He slid his hands up her back and pressed her forward, crushing her breasts against him and bringing her close enough for a kiss. Electrifying was the only word to describe the touch of her mouth on his. He slanted his lips over hers and she responded back with a passion that enflamed him. Soft and curvy, she fit perfectly in his arms, and he held her close as he tasted her. She sighed and opened her mouth against his insistent tongue. He slid his own between her parted lips and Frenched her. His mouth wasn't the only part of his body that got busy. His cock attempted to drill a hole through his pants to the damp sex it could sense rubbing against it. His hands slid down her back to cup and knead her full bottom, a perfect handful for him to grab and bounce her with on his cock later.

Just as he'd decided it was time to strip her of her offensive clothes, the damned phone rang.

"Ignore it," he muttered against her mouth.

"I can't. It could be work. Don't worry. I'll be right back, and I'll make it up to you." She slid off him, and, with a sultry look, wandered away to answer her phone.

She took her phone into the other room with a wink and Mictain sighed, leaning back into the couch. His cock strained, and given how things were going, he didn't think it too presumptuous to unbutton for a little relief.

"I see things are going well?"

Mictain jumped up and bit his tongue, barely managing to restrain his bellow of surprise. Lucifer stood behind the couch with a leer on his face. "What are you doing here?" hissed Mick.

"Checking on your progress. I see operation 'Get in her pants' is going well. If I'd known how hot the witch was, I might have taken the mission myself."

Mictain held back a growl even as jealousy flared in him at Lucifer's words. "You need to get out of here before she comes back." *And before the sight of Satan in her living room ruins the mood—and my chances of getting lucky.*

"I'm going. I just wanted to remind you that this isn't about pleasure, but about getting information. Try working on that before all the blood in your brain ends up in your dick."

Too late, thought Mictain. However, Lucifer's presence was a sobering—and prick shrinking—reminder that this wasn't a pleasure date.

"I'll find out what you want to know. Now get out." Mick knew he sounded grumpy, and Lucifer smirked before he popped out of sight, the lingering scent of brimstone making Mick groan. How was he supposed to hide that telltale calling card? He peered around the room and spied an incense holder. A match flare later and some cloying perfume filled the air, masking the scent of Hell.

He'd just thrown himself back on the couch when Marigold returned with a sultry smile, and Mictain really had to remind himself he was on a mission. Not an easy feat, especially when she dropped to her knees between his thighs, bringing her eye level with his rapidly expanding cock.

"Where were we?" she mused as she ran a finger down the crotch of his jeans.

"You know, I don't really know anything about you. How old are you? Do you have any family? Are you seeing someone?" What Mictain actually wanted to know was could she deep throat his cock and did she squirt when she came?

"I never knew my father. My mother is dead. I'm a twenty-five-year-old working witch. And I already told you I wouldn't have invited you over if I was seeing anyone. Satisfied?" She braced her hands on his thighs and nudged his shirt up with her nose until she bared the skin on his lower abdomen. She pressed her mouth to him and Mictain fought to hold on to his sanity.

He swallowed. "So, um, have you always been able to see things?"

Marigold, who had moved her mouth down to his jeans and was using her teeth to pull down his zipper, paused to eye him strangely. "If you're asking if I see ghosts then the answer is no." She resumed the invasion of his pants, and he dug his nails into his palms to keep his eyes from rolling back in his head when she placed her hot mouth on the thin layer of cotton that covered his shaft.

"Oh fuck, um, so what can you see that other people can't?" he gasped, rapidly losing his train of thought.

"I can see that you have a really fucked up idea of dirty talk," she said, pausing her oral play to eye him.

"Just trying to get to know you b-b-better," he stuttered as she freed his cock with her hand and stroked it. The witch had him incoherent and holding on to the barest edge of sanity, and he didn't understand his out of proportion reaction to her touch even as he loved it.

"Here, get acquainted with my mouth then," she said before inhaling him in one long stroke.

Mictain bit his tongue, the pain keeping him from shouting and blowing his load. It had been much too long since he'd assuaged his lust. *I shouldn't lie to myself. It's Marigold causing this insane reaction. I just don't understand why or how.*

He gazed down at her head bobbing up and down on his dick and promptly forgot his next question. He stared up at the ceiling and breathed deep. *I am a god. Surely I can handle a blowjob.*

"Um." He swallowed as she took him down to the root. "Yeah, so why do you think you, um, have this special power to see me?" Mictain hated himself for sounding like a complete fucking idiot. *I'm a god for fuck's sake, yet here I am trying to pump a witch for information instead of pumping her for pleasure.*

The wet sucking sounds stopped and his rod slid out of her mouth with a moist plop.

"What's with the twenty questions? If I didn't know better, I'd think you were grilling me for info."

Mictain couldn't stop a blush from heating his cheeks. "Of course not. Just trying to get to know you better." He recognized his reply as weak even as he said it, and besides, his culpability was already evident on his face.

Marigold jumped up. "You bastard. You are looking for info. And here I thought you'd come to dinner because you felt the same connection between us that I did."

"I do. I'm not. I—" Flustered at his capture, Mictain tried to collect his thoughts, but with most of his blood still centered in his groin, he was having a hard time.

"I can't believe I had a Brazilian done for you."

"Brazilian?" Wasn't that when a woman ended up pretty much clean shaven down below? Mictain cursed Satan. Cursed his ineptitude. And cursed himself for not fucking her first and asking questions later. "Can I see?" Please. He'd do anything to regain the mood he'd ruined.

"Dream on, jerk. You've lost your chance to see and play with this smooth pussy. Now why don't you get out and don't come back."

Hands on her hips, Marigold stood in front of him, the steam almost literally bursting from her ears, and Mictain, glutton that he was, couldn't resist one last remark before popping back to Hades. "Damn, you're hot when you're mad."

The tossed remote only narrowly missed his head.

5

MARIGOLD SCREECHED and stomped her foot as Mick disappeared, leaving behind one very pissed off and sexually frustrated witch.

"Jerk," she muttered, flopping onto her couch. Such high hopes, dashed by his subterfuge. She should have been glad she'd caught onto his game before she'd fucked him, but honestly, given her aroused state, she wished he'd waited until after to reveal his intentions. Now, she'd have to manually pleasure herself, and after her fantasies of him all day, what a letdown.

And he was such a great kisser. She pouted. She'd looked forward to having those deft lips of his kissing her pussy. What about that marvelously huge cock of his? What she wouldn't give to have its thick length penetrating her, pumping, taking her to nirvana.

These kinds of thoughts did nothing to abate her arousal. On the contrary, she found herself hornier than ever. Marigold skimmed a hand down her body and hunched up her dress so she could slide her hand between her thighs. She stroked the wet crotch of her panties, but it wasn't enough. She pushed the fabric aside and slipped her finger right into her aroused sex.

Too small. She slid in a second finger and a third, but remembering the thick feel of his cock in her mouth—and length, oh my—she remained dissatisfied. She rubbed at her clit with honey-slicked fingers and closed her eyes. She imagined his dark head between her thighs, his agile tongue lapping between her moist lips and flicking against her clit.

She squirmed on the couch, masturbating to a mental fantasy of him giving her a good tongue rub down. It felt good, but it couldn't compare to the real thing. After a while, she gave up and pounded at her couch pillows. It sucked to be horny and unable to do anything about it.

If he weren't already dead, I'd kill him again for leaving me like this. Right after I used him for sex of course.

MICTAIN ARRIVED BACK IN HELL MORE CONFUSED THAN ever, and aroused beyond belief. The way Marigold had sucked him—damn, the witch had talent. But, his attraction to her went past just chemical lust. She also intrigued him and drew him like no other woman, ever. And that said a lot. He'd bedded his fair share of attractive women, gorgeous women with perfect figures and flawless features, yet something about this freckled witch with the soft and plentiful curves drew him and shredded his control. It made no sense.

A lust spell? The power required to affect one of his stature was more than her tempting human body could channel, but what did that leave?

True love?

Mictain laughed aloud. He'd lived thousands of years, most of them alone. There was no way he could be falling in love with a witch, and a human at that. How then to explain why he found himself itching for her presence? Wondering what she did. If she thought of him too. If she touched...

On second thought, he could take a peek. Where was that app on his phone that allowed him to keep tabs on his clients? It didn't take long to load, and what he saw sent him sinking onto his couch.

Cheeks flushed and eyes closed, Marigold touched herself. She'd hiked her skirt and bared her sex, revealing its smooth state. He groaned as he saw her slick fingers working that sweet pussy. Drooled for a taste of the moisture coating her digits. Almost popped back into her apartment to beg her forgiveness and give her what she so obviously needed.

She needs me.

But he'd blown his chance. He shut down the app, feeling like an even bigger jerk for having spied on her. *My own fault for listening to Lucifer.* Speaking of whom...

With a curse, Mick punched in the number to call his boss only to have the lord of Hades appear in front of him, a huge smirk on his face.

"Mictain, my old friend, how truly inept of you. You left the poor girl hornier than a herd of nymphos."

"You were watching?" Mictain didn't feel embarrassed.

He found an audience that he knew about—could enhance the fucking experience. Although, he had a feeling Marigold probably wouldn't view someone spying on them doing the naughty tango in quite the same titillating light. Not that it mattered anymore. She'd kicked him out and didn't want to see him again, which was for the best. *Besides, there's plenty of other pussy in the sea.*

"Of course I watched. Lord of sin, remember?" Lucifer grinned and waggled his brows. "And you and that witch were definitely sinning. But really, Mictain, I shouldn't have to tell you to make sure you finish your *business* before jumping all over her for intel." Satan mimed holding some hips and thrusting his groin.

Mictain groaned and slumped on his couch. "Why do I ever listen to you? Well, you can forget her telling me anything now." And her agreeing to go on a second date, because despite her throwing him out, Mictain wanted to see her, touch her, be with her, more than ever, and he was damned if he could figure out why, and at this point, how.

"Turns out I didn't need your amateurish attempt at sleuthing. I found out why she can see you," replied Lucifer smugly.

"And?"

"She's not quite human."

"So what is she?" Mictain perked up at the news. Perhaps he'd get an explanation for his attraction to her.

"Oh no. I'm not giving you the answer. You want to know so bad, you figure it out yourself. Needless to say, I've taken her off the death roster for the moment. I owed her father a favor."

"Who's her dad?" Mictain fished.

"Wouldn't you like to know?"

"Actually, I would."

"Well, too bad. I promised I wouldn't tell, and we all know I am a man of my word."

Mictain choked. "Since when?"

"Since her father and I came to an agreement." With a diabolical grin, Lucifer disappeared in a puff of smoke, the stench of brimstone making Mictain cough.

Great, now I don't need to see her anymore and pump her for info. For some reason, losing his reason to see her didn't cheer him, and neither did his fist pump in the shower to relieve the pressure in his groin.

6

"SUCKER!" Lucifer chuckled, an evil chuckle of course, as if there was any other acceptable kind. He did so love it when he managed to pull off subtle wickedness. The satisfying feeling. The giddy anticipation as he waited for his plot to unfold. The—

He yelped—in a very un-Satan like manner—as an unexpected voice inquired, "Who did you screw over now?"

Clutching at his chest, he glared at his girlfriend. "Fuck, woman. Give me a heart attack, why don't you."

"You'd need a heart for that," was her dry response.

"A waste of an organ, if you ask me. Another liver so a male can drink more alcohol, now that would have made more sense."

She shook her head. "You are such a man. And you didn't answer my question. Who did you screw this time?"

"Screw is such a harsh term."

"Oh for earth's sake. Would you answer the bloody question? I know you popped off to visit your nemesis."

"Were you spying on me, woman?"

Unabashed at having gotten caught, she replied, "Yes."

"You know, stalking is considered a sin."

"I know. How turned on are you now?"

"Very," Lucifer growled. He prowled over to the couch she lay sprawled on, but she evaded his roaming hands—even the extra pair he called into existence.

Holding him at bay with her own magic, she engaged him in conversation of all things, and not of the sexual kind.

"Since you think you're so clever, why don't you guess what I did?" A plot so diabolical only he could have come up with it.

"You made a deal with Marigold's father, who also happens to be the favored competitor in the upcoming golf match."

"Give the woman a prize!" he shouted. "Oh wait. You've already got the biggest prize of all. Me!"

"Why do I feel so robbed?" Gaia ruefully shook her head.

"Ha. Very funny. Not. You know you adore me."

"Like a tick loves spring. So what did you get her daddy to promise?"

"Oh not much."

"I find that hard to believe."

"Believe it, woman. Seems he's more concerned about keeping his love child a secret from his wife than trying his hardest in the upcoming golf match."

"Cheating again?" she asked with an arched brow.

"Blackmail isn't cheating."

"How do you figure that?"

"Because I said so and I'm the lord of sin."

"So what did you do?"

"Well, you know my plan to get Mictain and Marigold together to make me super babies?"

"Yes."

"After I got him to promise at least two bogey holes, I kind of revealed to her daddy they were dating."

"You mean having sex?"

"One and the same. Apparently, he'd not kept dibs on her recently. His spies have somehow gone missing."

"Which you know nothing about, of course."

"Who, me?" He batted his lashes and she snorted. "Anyhow, daddy is not happy about it and has vowed to put a stop to it."

"How is that good? I thought you wanted Marigold and Mictain together as part of your ultimate dating plan."

"I do. Is there anything stronger than forbidden lust?"

"Don't you mean love?"

"You say tomato, I say, fucking."

Her nose wrinkled adorably. "That makes no sense."

"That's because you're a woman."

"With a brain."

"Again, another wasted organ."

Gaia sighed. "You know, it's really not nice to toy with people's emotions. Poor Mictain is supposed to be your friend and yet here you are, dicking him around, along with that poor girl."

"I know. Marvelous, isn't it?"

A giggle escaped her. "You are utterly incorrigible."

"Yes. Yes, I am. I am also sinfully delicious. Wanna taste?"

Lucky for him, she did, and somewhere on earth, a volcano erupted.

7

EVEN AFTER SLEEPING ON IT, Marigold remained pissed, and horny. *Stupid jerk.* And even stupider her. She'd thought Mick genuinely liked her. Instead, he'd wanted to know why she could see him. As if she had a clue.

Since a young age, Marigold knew she was special. Not many children could levitate objects, or set things on fire, or see spirits. Given some of her strange abilities—which for lack of a more scientific term, she labeled magic—she even hypothesized she was perhaps not completely human. What DNA ran through her, though, remained a mystery. Her mother, whom she loved dearly, was a bit of a ditz. Blonde, giggly, and with not a serious thought in her head, she'd worked on a cruise line for years before having her and had no recollection of Marigold's father other than he was handsome. Not even a name. Even stranger was despite her lack of memories, her mother refused to date anyone since in the off chance her mystery lover came back.

Like that ever happened. Whoever her dad was, he'd disappeared into the blue yonder and never looked back.

It used to bother Marigold; after all, who didn't want to know where they came from? What their roots were? But over the years, she'd adopted more of a screw him attitude. If he couldn't care enough to even contact her then he wasn't worth wasting a thought on.

Mick's questions, though, resurrected a long-buried curiosity. *Who was my father? Actually, the better question is what was my father?*

It also made her wonder what super powers she might have inherited other than those she knew about and her most recent ability to spot death. *Which, on second thought, could be a totally cool ability. I could hire myself out to rich folk and protect them from death itself.*

Of course, first that would entail convincing people she even had the power to do that. *But, at least I might see Mick again.*

Marigold groaned in frustration. It figured her horny libido would circle back to him. The guy was scum. A user. A totally hot piece of ass that she wanted to jump so badly.

That's it. There's only one cure for what ails me—another man. A rebound lover, so to speak.

"Tonight, after work, I'm going out and finding myself a nice, no-strings-attached man." She spoke aloud, which was stupid since there was no one there to hear her.

Despite her determination, though, she spent all day thinking of Mick—naked.

Waking the next day—after having spent the night dreaming about a freckled witch—Mictain found himself at a loss with what to do with himself. Until he'd solved the Marigold mystery, Lucifer had suspended his usual soul-collecting duties. And while, Lucifer had actually figured it out himself, he'd not had Mictain reinstated in the soul collection roster. An oversight Mictain didn't plan to correct.

However, the extra time on his hands did nothing to help him decide his next move. After the sour note he and Marigold had ended things on the night before, it might prove awkward to just show up as if nothing happened. *Maybe if I brought chocolate or flowers, she would forgive me?* Or slam the door in his face.

He could just storm her apartment, draw her into his arms, kiss her breathless and then proceed to seduce her body. On second thought, while that really worked for him, she might not appreciate him manhandling her, especially if she was still mad.

He needed advice. Dating advice, and not from Lucifer, the world's greatest seducer—and most reviled ex-boyfriend of females universe wide—but from someone with a little bit of respect for women. A man whose previous paramours still greeted him with a smile and come-hither glances.

Given the time of day, he doubted he'd find Felipe at the bar where he worked as a bouncer. When calls to his cell phone and apartment went unanswered, Mictain headed over to the gym his friend liked to frequent. Sure enough, Felipe was working out, or so he assumed by the bevy of females standing around staring and tittering.

Shirtless and muscles straining, the male who could shape-shift into a three ton hellcat didn't seem oblivious to the attention.

"Got a minute?" Mictain asked his friend when he stopped doing reps with the barbell to mop his brow.

"Sure. Why don't we hit the men's sauna?"

An audible sigh of disappointment swept through the gathered women, and Mictain restrained himself from snorting. *How does he do it?* The guy must have some kind of a cock or technique to inspire such a reaction.

Stripping first in the locker room, they each wrapped a towel around their loins for modesty's sake. The sauna let out a puff of steam when they entered, and sweat immediately formed on his body. Mictain flopped onto the wooden bench with a heavy sigh.

"Dude, you look seriously bummed. Is the boss man running you ragged again with plagues?"

"No. Worse. He wants me to seduce a woman."

Felipe choked—with laughter. "Excuse me. I think I heard you wrong."

"Doubtful. As fucked up as it sounds, I'm to get close to a mortal witch and find out how come she can see me when I'm wearing my reaper cloak."

"So ask her."

"I did. She didn't know. The boss thinks she's hiding the truth so he thought if I seduced her, I could get her to open up and tell me."

"And you came to me for tips? Dude, don't tell me it's been so long you've forgotten how?" Felipe chortled and slapped his thigh.

A frown knitted Mictain's brows together. "I haven't

forgotten I was doing perfectly fine until Lucifer showed up."

Felipe howled louder. "You had an audience. This is getting better and better."

"Not really. I went from almost getting head to getting kicked out because she caught on to the fact I was pumping her for information."

"Oh, dude. That is rotten luck."

"No kidding. So here's my dilemma. I still want to get that info, but she's pissed at me."

"No problem, my friend. I will seduce the witch and get the answer you seek."

"Like fuck!" He shouted the refusal, and Felipe arched a brow. Mictain tried to shove his sudden anger back down. He didn't understand where it came from. The offer was perfectly reasonable, even generous given Felipe had never met Marigold, yet, it didn't sit well with him at all. The thought of Felipe kissing her and touching— Mictain clenched his fist lest he lash out. Jaw tight, he said, "This is my assignment and my fuck up. I'll take care of it. What I need from you is advice on how to get her to forgive me."

"Apologize."

"With jewelry, chocolate, or flowers? Or should I do all three?"

"Why don't you try with words?"

"You mean tell her I'm sorry? No way." Mictain shook his head. "That seems too simple. No way is it going to work."

Spreading his hands, Felipe shrugged. "Hey, you asked. I'm just telling you what I'd do."

"Does it work for you?"

"Don't know. I don't usually piss off my lovers in the midst of getting a BJ."

The reminder deflated Mictain. "Any more advice?"

"If you like this girl, then just follow your instincts. Forget about what Lucifer wants. Trust yourself."

"I never said I liked her."

Felipe shot him a wry smile. "You didn't have to. Your actions speak for themselves."

Really? Then he wished they'd speak more clearly to him because he didn't know what to make of the emotions one fragile mortal inspired. Not completely true. The lust she engendered he could easily solve—between her thighs or lips. It was the rest of it, the possessiveness that reared its head and the urge to see her again that didn't make sense. Like her? It seemed too simple of an explanation.

Great. Now I have a second mystery to solve. And a second surprise date to prepare for.

8

"WHAT DO YOU WANT?" Marigold spoke brusquely to hide her shock—and yes, pleasure—at seeing Mick again. Of course, she'd have felt more on even ground had she not just gotten out of the shower wearing only a towel, a state he seemed to enjoy judging by the bulge growing at his groin.

He grinned at her, not at all put out by her not-so-warm welcome. "Aren't you glad to see me?"

Actually, she was happy he'd come back, which really annoyed her. "Gee, let me see. Happy to see a guy who faked interest in me so he could get head and information? Screw off." Marigold went around him into her bedroom, but like most pests, he wouldn't leave.

"Listen, I am sorry about that. I was under orders from the big man himself."

"Yeah, well, bully for you. Now if you don't mind, I need to get dressed." Marigold stared at him boldly and when he didn't leave, she dropped the towel. She smirked at his dropped jaw and then turned to dig through her closet for something to wear.

"You really aren't like other women, are you?" he said, a hint of wonder in his tone.

She ignored him, although she considered his words a compliment. She prided herself on her unique nature. She stepped into a skimpy g-string, her movements more sensual than usual. Having him watch her dress was having a disturbing effect on her libido—in other words, she was wet and not from the shower. Pissed that even after she'd pegged him for a using piece of scum, she wanted him, she decided to screw with him by turning to face him while she hopped, pulled, stretched, and squirmed into a tight pair of leather pants. The look on his face was priceless, although his smoldering eyes made her want to yank down her pants and scream, "Take me!"

Her nipples hardened at her dirty thoughts and he licked his lips, his eyes riveted to them. *Men!* She skipped her bra to wear an almost sheer top that tied around her neck and upper torso like a bikini top, leaving her back and midriff bare. The material also clearly outlined her erect nubs.

"Um, where are you going dressed like that?" he asked, his brows beetling into a frown.

"Out." She leaned over her dresser to peer into the mirror as she applied her makeup.

"No, you're not," he stated sternly. "Not dressed, or should I say *undressed*, like that."

Marigold, her lipstick poised in front of her mouth, gazed at his reflection in the mirror and snorted. "You can't give me orders." *But damn you're hot when you're acting jealous and possessive.*

"It's not an order. More of a request."

"And the answer is still no."

"Is it because I didn't bring flowers or chocolate?"

She snorted. "You can't buy forgiveness."

"I hear some men do with diamonds."

"I don't wear jewelry."

"You really aren't going to make this easy."

"Why should I? I'm not the one who pretended to like someone just so I could gather information."

"Does it help if I admit I wasn't pretending?"

Yes. Her heart fluttered, but she held firm. "No. Now, if you don't mind, please leave. I have plans to go out."

He barred her way. "Listen, I came here to make things up to you. Can't we just stay in and...*talk?*"

For a moment, she allowed herself to picture his mouth having an intimate conversation with her lower set of lips. Her sex quivered and she mentally shook herself. *Down, pussy. We'll get some action soon.* At his expectant look, Marigold uttered a full-throated laugh. "Talk? Oh please, I wasn't born yesterday. You can forget a repeat oral performance. I am going out whether you like it or not, and if I'm lucky, I'll be the one getting a tongue lashing," she said with a wink. Pushing past him, she dug through her front hall closet for a pair of heels.

She left her apartment with him trailing after her, a big, dark masculine presence that made her almost reconsider. *We could stay home, and I could let him prove to me just how sorry he is. I bet he'd look great on his knees pleasuring me. And over me, fucking me hard. And...*

Marigold scowled. *No, I am not falling into his seductive trap again.* He'd fooled her once into thinking he liked her. She wouldn't fall for it a second time.

Her high heels clacked on the pavement as she headed toward the club a few blocks from her place, which she frequented every so often when she needed to blow off steam.

"So, where are we going?" he asked, flashing her a white smile.

She scowled at him. "Go away."

"Nope."

She tried to ignore him, but her pussy wouldn't, and a throbbing started below her waist. In her tight pants, she couldn't feel the moisture, but she'd just bet it was there, dammed in her sex and waiting for an eager mouth to gush onto.

Faster she walked, and the jerk, as if he knew, laughed, his rich baritone making her shiver. He mistakenly believed it was her lack of a coat causing the chill and he draped an arm around her, tugging her into his body. He was hot, and not just in the good-looking sense. His whole body radiated heat and she didn't pull away. It felt too damn good.

All too soon they reached the lights and noise of the club. She slipped out from the warm cocoon of his arm, the cooler air making her want to duck back into him. Head high, and hips swishing, she strode up to the doorman manning the lineup. The gorilla in a t-shirt and jeans smiled when he saw her.

"Hey, Mari. Did you bring me the stuff?"

Marigold returned Frank's smile and handed him a

package. They'd come to an agreement a while ago. She gave him a free tonic to keep his bald pate hairless and shining, and he let her into the club whenever she wanted no matter how long the lineup.

Before stepping through the doors, she turned and blew a kiss to Mick, stuck outside with the other wanna-be clubbers. *Frank will never let him through.* For some reason her spirits sank and she sternly told herself it wasn't disappointment at the knowledge she'd managed to lose Mick for the night.

Forget him. There are plenty of other men who are just looking for the same thing I am—a good time. Turning her back on him, she resolved to have fun—and forgot he existed.

Marigold let the noise and heat of hundreds of bodies thrashing to music flow over her. The hard, heavy beat proved hard to resist, and she gyrated her way onto the dance floor already crowded with writhing people. In no time at all, a male body brushed up against her rear, and tingles shot through her. *Damn, I must be really fucking desperate to get aroused just from the touch of a sightless stranger.*

She kept dancing, waggling her bottom at her unseen partner, whose brief touches set her blood boiling. She'd get a look at him when the song ended and see if he met her visual requirements. In other words, not paper-bag-ugly. She didn't care if he was interesting, smart, or rich. She just wanted to get laid, and judging by the tingles, she'd found her guy.

The song wound down, but before she could twirl and eyeball her partner, a muscular arm snaked around her waist and a familiar voice whispered, "This would have been a lot more fun naked."

No freaking way. Marigold broke Mick's hold and turned to glare at him. "Will you go away? Guys will think I'm taken if you hang around me."

"Exactly," he said unabashedly.

With a sigh of exasperation, Marigold pushed past him to the bar. She needed a drink, a large one right now. The bartender, who also knew her, handed her a frothy piña colada replete with an umbrella and cherry. Marigold took the drink with thanks and then turned to lean her back against the bar as she sipped. She almost choked.

Mick hadn't followed her to the bar. Oh no, the sexy bastard who'd set her blood on fire danced with not one, not two, but three bimbos! Marigold simmered even as she knew her jealousy was unreasonable. *So much for him wanting me. That jerk seems awfully happy surrounded by those sluts. Good, that means he won't bother me anymore.*

Marigold forced herself to look away, but couldn't stop the anger, and inexplicable jealousy. Determined to prove to him—and herself—that she didn't care, she grabbed the nearest man and dragged him out to dance. She intentionally faced away from Mick and dirty danced with her new partner, who grinned at his stroke of luck.

With a critical eye, Marigold took stock—early twenties, good teeth, decent build. All in all, a decent sort. Unfortunately, he wasn't Mick. No matter, she'd make do. She rubbed herself on the blond stranger and then flipped to spoon dance him. This gave her a direct view of Mick, who stood still, glaring at her across the dance floor.

Pleased she'd gotten his attention, she smirked and ground her ass harder against her dance partner.

When Mick began pushing at people in a straight beeline toward her, his face a dark thundercloud, she debated waiting for him, but then thought better of it. She grabbed her guy's hand and dragged him to the exit.

"Hey baby, where we going?"

"Let's get some fresh air."

"Sounds *good*." The guy's inflection left no doubt as to what he thought she meant, however, Marigold had no intention of screwing the stranger she dragged out of the club. Not anymore. Despite his decent looks, something about him repelled her, and she always trusted her instincts. Hell, under normal circumstances, she would have never led him to believe she was interested. She did, however, want to antagonize Mick by making him think she was. A great plan until she got outside with the blond Ken doll and he suddenly turned into Mr. Grabby. She slapped at his hands and dodged a sloppy kiss.

"What's wrong with you?" he demanded angrily.

"I changed my mind," she retorted, and turned to walk away. But Mr. Grabby apparently didn't grasp that no meant no. He clamped thick fingers around her arm to stop her from leaving. Marigold dug her hand into her purse and flung some magic powder in his eyes, her version of pepper spray.

Unfortunately, he didn't react like a normal man would. Then again, that might have had a lot to do with the fact he wasn't human!

Holy freaking moly!

Her blond Ken doll shed his human guise kind of like

the alien in *Men in Black*. He sloughed off his human skin off to reveal a very ugly creature dressed still in jeans and a t-shirt strategically ripped to allow its spines to poke through. With horns protruding from his forehead and the red glow of his eyes, it didn't take a genius to point out she'd just met her very first demon.

Marigold lost a few precious seconds to shock. After all, it wasn't everyday she ran into a denizen of Hell. By the time she ordered her feet to run, the demon had already grabbed a hold of her and leered. Or grimaced, it was hard to tell with all the pointy teeth and hanging drool. *Eew, no wonder he hides behind a mask.*

"Give me a kiss, baby," it hissed, flicking out a forked tongue.

"Oh, like, no bloody way," she said, unable to stop the disgust in her tone.

"Teasing slut," it roared before pitching her. Marigold had a moment to enjoy flying for the first time before she crashed into a wall hard and slumped down, spots dancing before her eyes.

Dazed, she could only sit on the ground and watch as two sets of blurry legs approached and stopped in front of her. For a moment, she wondered if the demon had cloned itself. She blinked and her double vision cleared. That was better, only one pair of legs. Her ears rang, but even through that annoying sound and the nausea churning her stomach, she had no trouble recognizing the sound of a zipper lowering.

That doesn't sound good.

9

MICTAIN DIDN'T ARRIVE in time to stop Marigold's impromptu flight and intimate encounter with the wall, but he was behind the demon when it yanked down its zipper.

"Like bloody hell," growled Mictain. "Get away from her."

The ugly pit demon whirled, its red eyes glaring at him. "This doesn't concern you," it hissed.

"Wrong. The girl is mine." Mictain enjoyed saying the possessive words.

"Stupid human. I shall enjoy killing you." The demon grinned with pointed teeth and slimy drool.

He probably meant to appear scary, but Mictain laughed. He hung out with a lot worse back home. "Who said I was human?" Mictain then proceeded to show the beast the error of its ways. As an Aztec god, Mictain was far from normal. He was stronger, faster, and at his core, a natural born warrior, and of course, a god. A demon of the lower castes wasn't even close to a match. With a few well-aimed blows, Mictain incapacitated the creature who thought to hurt his woman and sent him back to Hell for punishment. Lucifer frowned upon demons who preyed on the mortals for fun. Lucifer enjoyed explaining to breakers of this rule, usually with a sharp object, that the torture of mankind was his job.

Danger taken care of, he turned his attention to Marigold, still ignobly splayed on the pavement, her eyelashes fluttering. He scooped her up with care then strode out of the alley and toward her apartment.

"You with me, witch?" He suspected she'd sustained a concussion and wanted to keep her awake if possible.

"Dat wasss hot," she slurred against his chest.

"I know I am. Silly witch. What were you thinking?" She didn't answer, though. Her eyes shut and her head lolled against him. His anger burned at her injury and he wanted to bring the demon back so he could beat the fuck out of it again. *How dare he touch my woman.*

He called for his reaper cloak, enveloping them within its folds and rendering them invisible. Or so he hoped. For all he knew, Marigold's very presence would annul its magic. Not that he cared at this point; her wellbeing was more important than a few pointed stares from humans. He picked up his speed and ran with her cradled in his arms, his legs swiftly eating up the few yards left to her apartment. He charged up the stairs and zipped down the hall to her apartment door.

He ran into a dilemma, though; her place was locked. It occurred to him that he could quite easily kick her door in, but not only would that possibly alert her neighbors, he didn't think Marigold would appreciate it. *Although, I'd like to know when I started caring about what a woman thinks.* Then again, as his cock reminded him, a happy woman was easier to get naked.

Kneeling, he balanced Marigold on one knee while he dug her key out of her little clutch purse still attached to a loop on her pants. He unlocked and opened the door before standing back up with her and going in. The door thumped as he kicked it shut behind him. He headed with the still unconscious Marigold to her bedroom. He just wished his first visit to her room could have been for other reasons—unclothed, sweaty ones.

Mictain walked into the pink nightmare for the second time that night and fought not to recoil. It hadn't improved in his absence. For a witch with a saucy sense of humor, her room was awfully girly. From the light pink walls to the darker comforter, everything was in shades of rose with the white furniture providing the only contrasting color. Hoping it wouldn't affect his masculinity, he placed her gently on her bed, then scratched his balls in an effort to combat the cloying femininity surrounding him.

Manliness reaffirmed, he knelt beside her on the bed and checked her pulse. A strong beat met his fingertips, reassuring him somewhat. He palpated her head until he found the goose egg on her scalp. She'd have a definite headache when she woke. He went to her kitchen and came back with a bag of frozen peas. He sat on the bed and lifted her on his lap before pressing the cold vegetable compress against her injury.

She didn't react. She lay still and it worried him.

"She's not going to die," said Satan, his voice sounding a few seconds before the scent of brimstone hit Mictain's nose.

"What are you doing here?"

"I got your present, thank you very much. Stupid demon. I gave him to her father to play with. There's one house that needs some ear plugs with all the screaming that's going on in the dungeon." Lucifer chuckled. "How come you're with the witch anyhow? Didn't you get my message saying I didn't need that information any more?"

"I did."

"And?"

"I decided to earn some brownie points disobeying a direct order."

For a moment, Lucifer appeared stymied. Then steam curled from his nose. "Defiance is only acceptable in other people's minions. I expect perfect obedience from mine."

"Oops. My bad. Now if you don't mind, I've got a witch to attend to."

"No, you don't. As I said, she won't die."

"Then it won't hurt if I stay and tend her."

"Oh it might. I didn't just come here to tell you that. I actually came on her father's behalf. He wants to know what the fuck your intentions are toward his daughter."

Intentions? Fuck if he knew. He'd not thought much past punishing the offending demon and then caring for her, healing her so he could without guilt peel off her clothes and claim her body with his. Probably not the answer he should go with. "Tell her father to ask me himself. Or better yet, tell me who he is and I'll tell him myself."

Lucifer grinned. "Nice try. I'm not going to give that bit of knowledge away that easily. But seriously, you never did answer me. Why are you back here with the chit? I told you I didn't need any info and she's off the soul claiming roster."

"Did it ever occur to you that what I do is none of your business?"

"No."

Despite his evil ways, Lucifer did have an odd sense of honesty. Mictain restrained a smile. "She intrigues me. You of all people should know how rare that can be."

"Rare, yes, but keep in mind that if you get involved and then decide later to break her heart, I won't stop her father from coming after you. A father's got the right to protect his little girl."

"Oh please," said Mictain, rolling his eyes. "She doesn't even know who her father is so I highly doubt he's as interested as you say. Not to mention Marigold is a grown woman. I'm sure I won't be her first lover."

"You could be her last, though," muttered Satan enigmatically. "Well, it was nice chatting, but I need to be off. I hear we're getting a whack of Taliban fighters and boy will they be surprised to meet me." With a poof, Lucifer went back to Hell and his job of meting out punishment with a smile.

"Was the devil just in my bedroom?" asked Marigold, her voice groggy.

He glanced down and saw her peering at him with bleary eyes. He smiled. "Hey, gorgeous, nice to know you have a thick head to go with your—"

"Don't even say it," she growled, clarity returning

quickly to her eyes. She pushed herself up from his lap only to groan and grab at her head. She collapsed back into his arms—where she belonged.

"I'd stay still if I were you. You've got a doozy of a bump on your head. Didn't your mother ever teach you not to play with demons?"

"She must have skipped that chapter when she read me *Dealing with Demons.*"

Relived she didn't seem worse for wear, Mictain chuckled. "What a lame joke. You must be feeling better."

"I will if you get me some bloody Tylenol. Bathroom cabinet, second shelf."

Mictain eased out from under her and went to fetch the medicine along with a glass of water. She popped the pills in her mouth and gulped the water gratefully. "Thanks. You can go now," she said, closing her eyes.

Ignoring her order, Mictain climbed onto her bed. Her eyes popped open and she glared at him. Despite her dirty look, she didn't fight him when he picked her upper body up and draped her on his lap again.

"Why won't you leave?"

"You have a concussion. You can't be alone." Besides, he felt no burning desire to go anywhere else. Not unless she came with him. His attraction to her made no sense. His need to stay with her baffled him. But, he couldn't bring himself to go.

"Then I'll call a friend."

"Not necessary." Like hell she would call someone else.

"I don't understand you. What do you want from me?" She peered up at him, her brows drawn in puzzlement.

A good question he didn't have an answer for yet, but he gave it a shot. "A kiss?"

"Seriously? That's all you want?"

He heard the incredulity in her tone and grinned. "Are you saying I should have aimed for more?"

"No. So just a kiss and you'll go then?" Surely that wasn't disappointment in her tone?

A kiss for now, he thought. *But when you get better, baby, I'm going to caress every inch of your body and then some.*

MARIGOLD'S HEAD THROBBED, BUT NOT AS MUCH AS HER pussy. *One kiss and he'll leave. I'd better make sure it's a good one.*

Mick slid her off his lap. She wondered if perhaps he'd change his mind and leave. Nope. He covered her, his large body poised over hers, his arms supporting his weight. Marigold sucked in a breath. With nowhere to look but up, she found herself drawn into his gaze. His smoldering eyes made her squirm, her arousal rapidly overtaking her discomfort and leaving her with a different kind of pain. A pain he could heal.

He lowered his head slowly until he hovered, a hairsbreadth above her mouth. She waited, her pulse speeding up with anticipation. Her nipples tightened. Her sex clenched. And when she thought she would scream at him to hurry up, he kissed her.

How could I ever have thought any other man would do? She hated to admit it, but when Mictain kissed her, it was like no other embrace she'd ever experienced. It instantly set her on fire. It made her forget she was mad at him. It took the pain from her injury and transformed it into pleasure. It made her heart race—for him.

He embraced her tenderly, sweet and soft caresses that teased her. She could sense the passion he restrained. It hovered there just beneath the surface, and she wanted it. She wanted it to touch her.

As if he heard her silent plea, his kiss deepened, his tongue slipping into her mouth to dance with hers. His lower body sank to rest against her pelvis and she let her thighs part, encouraging him to nestle between them. He got the hint and in his new position, thrust his groin against her sex. Even through her tight pants, it was like a jolt of pure electricity shot through her.

She gasped against his mouth. He pulled away.

"Are you okay? Did I hurt you?" he asked, his eyes shadowed with concern.

Lips throbbing—both upper and lower sets—she could only stare at him. *What is it about him that makes me lose my mind?* "I'm fine. You've had your kiss. You can leave now." She spoke the words even as her body—and strangely, her heart—screamed in her mind for him to stay.

"I told you, I'm not going anywhere."

She refused to admit or give in to the pleasure his simple declaration shot through her. "But you said you would if I kissed you."

"I never said I'd leave. You asked what I wanted and, might I say, I now wished I'd asked for more than a kiss."

"Pig. Get out." Marigold tried to put some conviction in her words, but couldn't help the smile that curved her lips, especially when he grinned at her unabashedly.

"What, you want me to get out of my pants? Sure, but first, why don't I give you a hand taking off yours?"

Marigold smirked. "Good luck. These suckers are skin tight, and I'm in no shape to struggle with them. I'm injured, remember." She continued to smile as she laced her hands under her head, which barely hurt now thanks to the Tylenol…and Mick.

He rubbed his hands together. "I love a challenge. I take it I'm not allowed to slice them off you?"

She mock scowled at him. "I love these pants. Don't you dare rip one stitch."

He winked, and in one deft motion, unbuttoned and unzipped her pants, giving her stomach some much needed breathing room. Her pussy, however, felt more confined than ever. She tingled at the hot brush of his fingers as he grabbed the waistband on either side and tugged. Not far, her pants were glued on.

He frowned. "Put your legs together."

"Gee, most guys would ask me to spread them further," she joked. He laughed as she scissored them shut with a smirk. He tightened his grip on her waistband and pulled again. They didn't move much further, but he grinned in accomplishment anyway. Slow and methodical, he yanked, wiggled, and rolled her pants down, peeling her like some exotic fruit, one leaking honey juices.

His nostrils flared, and his joking countenance turned serious. "You are one hot witch, and I want you *so* bad."

Despite her anger with him, Marigold echoed that sentiment and decided to throw good intentions to the wind. "So stop your teasing and have me."

He removed her pants with a flourish, leaving her

nude from the waist down except for her skimpy, soaking wet, g-string. "You're hurt. It would be wrong of me to take advantage of you. Joking aside, I'm only stripping you to make you comfortable."

Marigold laughed. "You work as a Grim Reaper, and you're worried about hurting me? What if I said I want you, now, in bed with me naked?"

Her words flustered him and he turned away, proving his backside was just as sexy as his front. He spoke, still turned away. "If I get into bed with you now, there's no turning back or saying no. My honor and patience only go so far."

"Then you'd better have some decent stamina because I have a feeling I'm going to need more than one round."

The sound of ripping cloth was her only warning. He covered her body again, decadently naked. Before she could speak, his mouth claimed hers in a passionate kiss that stole her breath. She brought her hands up and circled them around his neck, clasping him to her. His forearms kept his full weight off of her, but he hovered low enough that her nipples, still covered by sheer fabric, brushed his chest. That friction was enough to make them rock hard.

His mouth left hers and swept a blazing trail down her neck. She gasped when his big hands grabbed her breasts and squeezed. Simple caresses, yet her body arched into his touch, completely afire. When his mouth caught one erect tip and sucked it through her top, she moaned. It felt so damned good.

She twisted her upper body, trying to push her tingling globe further into his mouth. His hands used that moment to slide under her body and pull at the ties that held her shirt on. A moment later, her top went sailing, baring her to his heated view.

"So pretty," he murmured. "And *mine.*" His lowly spoken, possessive claim sent a shiver racing through her. His hands caught her waist and as he bowed his head to suck her nipple in his mouth, he lifted her pelvis and ground his hips forward. Her flimsy g-string was no barrier and his cock rubbed against her, swollen and hot.

Her fingers grabbed at his hair, pulling and urging him to move lower. He chuckled as he kissed his way down her body.

"What an impatient little witch you are. Tell me what you want," he murmured, rubbing his face against her naked pubes still hidden by the panties she now hated.

"Lick me," she growled. "Taste me. Make me cum on your tongue then take me." The dirty words spilled from her. She heard him suck in a breath and then her panties were gone, replaced with his mouth.

Women could say what they wanted, but a man who knew his way around a pussy with his mouth was priceless. Contrary to masculine popular belief, oral pleasure took some skill and Mick had that in spades.

He explored her sex from her burgeoning clit to her wet slit. He stretched and sucked on her plump lips. He probed her with his tongue, lapping at her honey. He sucked, flicked, and tortured her bundle of nerves so much that she flexed her hips up off the bed, keening.

He thrust several fingers in her sex while he stroked her swollen clit with his tongue "Cum for me," he murmured against her engorged nub. His words sent her over the edge and she let out a long cry that went well with the rippling orgasm that left her weak and trembling.

Her channel was still quivering when he thrust into her with his thick, hard cock.

"Oh, Mick." She grabbed at his shoulders and held on as he stroked her, his prick moving slowly in and out of her. Her still quaking body returned to the brink almost immediately. With a moan of pleasure, she shattered again, her channel squeezing him tight.

With a groan, he pumped into her one last time and held himself inside, his hot seed spurting.

Then he collapsed on top of her, squashing her flat.

"Um, some help here," she wheezed.

He rolled off with a sated, masculine chuckle. Not far, though. He tucked her into him, his warm body better than any blanket, and with a smile, Marigold fell asleep.

10

MICTAIN WOKE WITH A SMILE. The reason was still pillowed against him, and his cock hardened at the sight of her curvy naked body.

Then deflated.

"Oh man, are you in trouble now," said Satan, who stood at the foot of the bed shaking his head at them.

"Go away," hissed Mictain.

"Why? She's awake and, besides, I thought you'd like warning that her father is not a happy camper right now."

Beside him, Marigold stiffened. Mictain sighed. *So much for morning sex.* Marigold sat up and tried to cover herself with her hands as she glared at the devil. "I have no father. Now get out of my bedroom. And next time you decide to visit, knock on the door like everyone else."

"Do you know who I am, little girl?" roared Lucifer, smoke drifting from his ears, his complexion turning from tanned to beet red—never a good sign.

"A pain in my ass who has messed up my morning," she shouted back with a lack of fear Mictain found entertaining even as he prepared to protect her from Lucifer's wrath. "I was planning on having some great wake up sex. Instead, you show up, without even a coffee, and piss me off."

Lucifer gaped at Marigold, an expression mirrored on Mictain's own face. *Damn, my witch has guts. Hopefully I can keep them intact because apparently, she still hasn't learned her lesson about messing with demons.* Mictain hopped out of bed and held his hands up.

"Let's all calm down here. I'm sure Lucifer was just anxious that we not be caught unaware, right, Lucifer?"

Lucifer just glared at him.

He turned away from Satan and restrained a smile at the sight of Marigold looking rumpled and grumpy, and way too delicious-appearing in bed. "And baby, don't worry, once he leaves, I will give you the best morning sex you could ask for."

She also glared at him.

So much for diplomacy first thing in the morning. "Fine. Duke it out. See if I care. I'm going to find some coffee." Mictain wandered out of the room, naked, and as he'd hoped, Lucifer followed him grumbling.

"If I didn't know her father personally, I'd tan her ass until she learned proper respect. I don't get it. She's a witch. I thought they were all supposed to worship me?" Lucifer sounded incredulous.

Slamming through cupboards looking for coffee, Mictain grunted in reply. When Lucifer was in this kind of mood, listening was his best bet.

"And you? What the fuck were you thinking? Didn't I warn you about getting involved with her?"

Mictain located a kettle and filled it with water before placing it on the stove. "You said not to break her heart."

"Ha, like that would happen," said Marigold with a snort, walking into the kitchen wearing a short silk robe and looking delicious. "We had sex. Get over it. It's not like it's happening again."

Mictain fumbled the mugs he pulled out. "What do you mean?"

"It's called a one-night-stand. I scratched my sexual itch. You scratched yours. End of story."

Anger bubbled in Mictain at her nonchalant dismissal of what they shared. "An itch? You compare the pleasure we both attained to a rash that needs scratching? You know what happened between us is more than that."

Marigold laughed. "Oh, ple-e-e-ase. Are you implying you're going drop to a knee right now and declare undying love? Not freaking likely. I'd expect this kind of crap from an angel, or even an employee of Venus, but a minion of Death? Seriously?"

Lucifer, watching their verbal sparring match, howled with laughter. "Oh, this is great. Hey, witch, I don't suppose you'd like a job down in Hell? I could use a lass with your kind of balls down there."

She sent him a shriveling glance. Lucifer clammed up and toned down his grin.

Mictain's cheeks burned. *So much for thinking we had a connection. She's right. We had sex—great sex. End of story. I am not groveling like some pathetic asshole. Hasta la vista, baby.*

Back Mictain popped into Hell, alone.

MICK LEFT MARIGOLD ALONE WITH SATAN WITHOUT SO much as a goodbye. Instead of making her glad, it rendered her sad, which in turn made her mad. She turned her ire on the cause for her morning's ill humor—a very tanned, forties-looking male with silver highlights who hummed as he stirred the dozen sugar cubes he'd dropped into his coffee.

Well he definitely doesn't look like I'd pictured. Where's the horns and yellow, slitted eyes?

He broke the silence first. "So, tell me about yourself," said the Lord of Hell, sipping his overly sweetened brew.

"Get out."

"When I'm ready," he replied calmly as he added even more sugar to his coffee.

"Why are you here anyways? What are you, like, Mick's keeper?"

"Mick's my friend and, as such, it's up to me to tell him when he's being an idiot."

Indignation made her say, "How's him hooking up with me stupid?" *Aren't I good enough for him?*

The Devil put his cup down, and his intense gaze focused on her, making her shiver. "Haven't you paid attention? Your father is against it."

Marigold crossed her arms and narrowed her gaze. "As if I care what he thinks. He abandoned me before I was even born. So why should I give a damn what he thinks?"

"Such a potty mouth. Are you sure you don't want a

job in the pit?"

"I'm sure. And don't change the topic."

"Ah yes. Your father. You should give a fuck about his wishes because of who he is," replied Satan enigmatically.

Marigold sighed as he answered evasively, and she finally posed the query burning her tongue. "Who's my father?"

"Finally, she asks me. He's important. He's deadly. And he wants to remain incognito for the moment," he said, shrugging.

"What!" Marigold exploded and to her shock, so did all the glassware in her kitchen. Stunned, she didn't speak for a moment.

Lucifer chuckled. "Daddy's little girl has a temper. Looks like you may have more powers than we knew about. He'll be pleased."

"You can't do this to me," grumbled Marigold.

"Do what?" asked the Devil blithely.

Marigold held in her frustrated screech. "Don't play dumb. You know what I'm talking about. Dropping hints about my father and then refusing to give me his name. I have a right to know."

"Your anonymity is your safety. Enjoy it. If it became known whose daughter you actually were, your life would be in danger."

"Blah, blah, blah," Marigold said to intentionally antagonize him, done talking to the king of cryptic messages.

She got her intended result when with a muttered, "Stupid girl," the lord of lies popped out of her kitchen and back to Hell where he belonged.

Marigold collapsed onto a chair and leaned her head

forward to rest in her hands. Her head pounded, more from the morning's adrenaline wakeup than her injury of the previous night. Marigold had always healed faster than a human, but feeling the back of her head, she couldn't deny that ability seemed to have increased in strength for there was no trace of the bump on her noggin and only a slightly sore spot left as a reminder.

However, her emotions and thoughts were in turmoil, and she didn't know where to start unraveling them. Did she begin with the way Mick had come to her rescue and then taken care of her, and not just carnally? He'd rescued her like some superhot hero and then tended her like some Chippendale turned nurse.

And then there was the sex. Amazing and mind-blowing were a few words that came to mind when she thought of the way he'd made her body sing. Even now, just thinking about it made her sated body wake and warm. While great sex would have been fine, and she might have indulged in it for a while, what she wasn't prepared to deal with was how he made her feel.

Gone less than ten minutes and she missed him like a crack addict missed their next fix. She wanted him, now, tomorrow, and a scary amount of ever-afters. *I can't have fallen in love. I barely know him. He's a god, for goodness sake, who collects souls for Death and drives me batty.* Yet, despite the reasoning against, she couldn't completely deny she felt something for him, and it wasn't just lust.

Pushing that dilemma into a corner, she focused instead on Lucifer and his enigmatic words. *Who and what is my father?* All the hints about his supernatural position and powers had her more curious than a room full of cats.

She also found his sudden interest just as baffling. *Since when does my deadbeat daddy give a damn? Although, it's interesting my father doesn't like my most recent choice of bed partner.*

Marigold was unabashedly lusty and had indulged in sex for quite some time now, and with quite a few men—and even one woman. Why had her phantom father not stepped forward before this to protest her choice of lovers? What had changed?

Mick. He was the key, obviously, since her life until now had been boring and uneventful. Then, she met Mick and next thing she knew, she was fighting off a demon, and Satan made his first visit, implying he'd return. The cloying stench of brimstone lingered as a reminder, and Marigold sighed. *I'll have to buy stronger air freshener if that's going to become a habit of his.* The idea of Satan coming for Sunday dinner finally had her giggling, and some of the tension eased in her.

But, what do I do next? The smart thing to do would be to forget Mick and get on with her life, thus avoiding visits from the lord of darkness and belated paternal threats.

However, Marigold didn't enjoy taking the easy path. And besides, by going against what her father and Satan wanted, she got something she wanted—Mick. *Who's off sulking in Hell. I guess I'd better think of a way to get him back.* After a shower, though, if she was going to make up with the man—er god—who'd taken up residence in her mind, and she grudgingly admitted her heart, she needed to wash the body parts she'd use to gain forgiveness. And pleasure.

11

MICTAIN JOGGED THROUGH HELLPARK, weaving around the towering pillars of red rock that towered amidst the gnarly, almost leafless trees. He needed the mindless adrenaline of exercise to forget the events of the morning.

Bloody Lucifer. It's his fault I'm sweating in Hell instead of naked on top of Marigold. Mictain didn't give a fuck who Marigold's father was. He needed her—in his bed, in his arms, in his life because Felipe was right. He liked her. It was the only explanation for how quickly she'd already taken up residence in his heart.

How pathetic am I? A god worshipped in blood and lives, mooning over a witch who doesn't want me. Of course, that didn't mean he'd surrender that easily. He'd give her the space she seemed to want, but the war to gain her heart was far from over. He'd pay her a visit later once she'd had a chance to cool down, and hopefully, come to miss him. *And if she's still cranky, I'll let my tongue talk to her other mouth until she cums around again and again.*

His hellphone, strapped to his hip, beeped, signaling an incoming text message. Mictain ignored it, not in the mood to work today, the prerogative of a retired god who worked to dispel boredom and not because he had to. However, ignoring the message was apparently not an option because the damned phone went ballistic, beeping nonstop until Mictain stopped jogging and grabbed it to peer at its screen.

You've got to be fucking kidding me. With a curse, he popped out of Hades and appeared on the mortal plain atop a building rooftop. The sudden change in temperature made him shiver as his sweaty body cooled, but he ignored the chill as he strode across the concrete surface toward the woman perched on the edge, poised to jump.

"Get your ass down off that ledge," he bellowed.

His shout startled Marigold and her arms windmilled wildly as she tried to keep her balance. In a heart-stopping flash, Mictain was at her side. He swept her off the precipice into the safety of his arms and hugged her tight.

Then he shook her. "What the fuck were you doing? Since when are you suicidal? Things aren't that bad, dammit."

"Hi," she said, and then she grinned impishly him. "Thanks for answering my call."

"What?" He stared at her with incomprehension for a moment before understanding dawned. "You mean you faked a suicide attempt just to get me back here?"

She nodded, and Mictain, his heart filling with happiness that she'd wanted him back, no matter her strange method, laughed. "How about I leave you a phone number so next time you can just call me?"

"How boring is that?" she teased, twining her arms around his neck. She made a moue of distaste and pulled back. "Eew. You're all sweaty." She narrowed her eyes and looked him up and down. "It better be from exercising, *alone.*"

"I was jogging, so you can get that jealous gleam out of your eye."

"I am not jealous," she huffed. "And don't go thinking just because I was trying to get your attention that this means anything."

"Then why call me?"

"Because contrary to what I said this morning, my itch still needs scratching."

"I'll scratch that and more. It's what boyfriends are for." Mictain acted cool, but her words made him want to rip the clothes from her body and sink himself into her glorious sex.

"Whoa. Slow down. I never said we were dating. That implies emotional involvement."

Mictain held his temper as he leaned against the concrete parapet and folded his arms. "So what are we then?"

"How about friends with benefits?" she said, sliding up to him and tracing a finger down his chest.

Not quite what I have in mind, but it's a start. "Fuck buddies, huh? Sounds good to me, but just so we're clear," he said, leaning forward so his mouth hovered barely an inch from hers, "I don't share."

"Neither do I," she said as she tiptoed up to brush her mouth across his. "So you'd better get a half dozen donuts when you get our coffee."

It took him a second to get her joke. She skipped out of reach, but not quick enough to avoid his swat on her ass. She giggled and turned to waggle her bottom at him. He lunged, but she danced away. "Nope. You don't get to play with these buns until you feed me. So get moving. And bring a blanket too."

"Yes, general," he replied with a salute. He'd let her think she could order him around, for now. There was time enough later to battle over who would wear the pants in their relationship, although his true preference was that they wear none and stayed naked in bed for at least the next decade or so. Of course, first, he'd have to change her mind about their relationship. Fuck friends indeed. Marigold was his whether she wanted to accept it yet or not.

Mictain planned his seduction as he jogged down the twelve flights of stairs to the street. He smiled at the cashier as he bought them two large café mochas along with a dozen donuts. He got hard when he quickly popped back to his place to grab a blanket for them to picnic on—and then fuck. He became enraged when he emerged onto the rooftop and saw Marigold fighting for her life.

How dare someone touch my woman!

MARIGOLD LEANED ON THE CEMENT PARAPET AS SHE looked down at the street. She saw Mick emerge from her apartment building, moving briskly to the coffee shop. She smiled, unable to stop the warm glow that suffused her. Her crazy plan to call Death had worked, although she'd been somewhat worried she might get one of Mick's co-workers. But her very own angel of death arrived, swooping in to save her from herself. Much as she wanted to remain aloof and just use him for good sex, she knew she was falling for him. Judging by his capitulation, it appeared like he might have already tumbled.

Not that he'd said any actual words, but then again, they hadn't really had time to talk much. Something she planned to rectify over coffee, donuts, and then during the afterglow of good sex.

Which, judging by the sudden stench of brimstone, might end up delayed. Marigold whirled, expecting a visit from the big man. She got a surprise instead. A not so good one, which was kind of ironic because how many people would prefer a visit from Lucifer?

"Holy shit." Her breathy expletive was heard by the five demons advancing on her, or so she assumed by their matching grins. Not a pretty sight, especially for the human in their path. "Looking for someone?"

"Are you Marigold?"

"Uh, no."

A nasty chuckle met her refutation. "Nice try, witch. Be a good girl and don't try to run. It will go harder on you if you do."

"What exactly is it that you want?"

"Blood. Pain. Mayhem. All three. My friends and I aren't picky."

They also didn't bathe judging by the malodorous scent wafting her way. "Listen. You really don't want to do this."

"Oh yes, we do," said the squattest of the demons, his dark green skin adorned with warts and pustules. "Your father's going to regret pissing us off."

"But I don't even know who my father is." Marigold wanted to scream in frustration. *When I find out who that deadbeat is, I'm gonna blister his ears until he goes deaf, and kick him in the shin for messing up my sex-life.* And punish him for the damage to her face because somehow, she doubted the menacing demons would treat her gently.

"Not our problem," it replied, approaching along with its companions.

"Stop where you are!" she ordered imperiously. "My boyfriend will be back any minute and you really don't want to piss him off."

"Then we'd better kill you quick."

With a squeak, Marigold dove to the side and away from the claws swinging at her. They still snagged on her shirt, tearing a hole, but at least it wasn't her skin. She ran, but there was nowhere to go. The door to the building was behind their advancing line, leaving her only with a choice of fight or a swan dive off twelve stories.

I just need to hold them off long enough for Mick to get here. He'll kick their asses for me! She might be a witch, but her powers lay in potions, not lightning bolts zapping from her fingertips. As for her newfound power to shatter glass, she tried to imagine the demons imploding to no effect.

Fast and tricky, it was what she needed to stay out of reach of a very painful death. A great plan against humans, but against demons, she didn't stand a chance. And they knew it.

They toyed with her, barking with guttural laughter as they spun her from one slimy grasp to another, their sharp claws leaving scratches that stung all over her body. Her vision blurred, and dizzy, she sank to the ground, unable to prevent her knees from buckling. Between the spined and scaled legs, she saw the door to the rooftop open. Coffee and donuts went flying as Mick charged at the group of demons with a fierce bellow.

"Bastards! You'll pay for your actions."

Pay how much? she wondered inanely. Marigold tried to keep her eyes open, she so wanted to watch her lover in action, but her lids fluttered shut against her will, pulled down as if cement blocks were tied to her lashes. She listened to the grunts and meaty smacks of Mick exacting vengeance. *Ha! Take that you nasty creatures.* She wished the muscles in her face would move so she could smile.

It took too much effort. Darkness beckoned and she allowed herself to slip in its numbing embrace.

FURY BOILED the blood in his veins. Gone only minutes to fetch his witch sustenance and he returned to find her getting pummeled. Unacceptable. Did they not know who they messed with? Did these lower caste demons not have any respect for their elders anymore?

They would once he was done with them. The demons who'd dared to touch *his* witch learned what it meant to raise the wrath of a god. He demolished them with his fists—meaty, bone-crunching blows no mortal creature could have withstood. His rage gave him extra strength, enough to rip limbs free and then swing them as a club, knocking the unworthy creatures around until they crawled, dripping ichor and blubbering for mercy.

As if he'd give them any.

Mictain dragged them back to face more of his justice, not satisfied until they cried, begged, and pleaded for death. Then, and only then, did he send them to Hell where he knew Lucifer would make them suffer some more. In his mind, an eternity wouldn't be enough, not for what they'd done to his Marigold.

Speaking of whom, she didn't look too healthy. He knelt at her side, wincing at the cuts and bruises blossoming all over the visible parts of her body. Gray of complexion and unconscious, he cursed as he realized her human side was reacting to the toxin from the demons' claws. He picked her up and cradled her carefully in his arms. He began heading toward the stairs leading down to her apartment when he realized Marigold wouldn't have the unguents and remedies needed to help her. *But I've got some back at my place where I can also keep her safe.*

However, his translocation magic didn't allow him to bring a passenger. Only a few demons could create a portal strong enough for more than one entity. Much as it galled him, he called upon his boss.

"Lucifer!" It might have appeared strange for him to call the Devil's name out loud, but no stranger than having a reply in the form of a kilt-wearing, bare-chested Lucifer wielding a golf club, wearing a tam with a cigar hanging out of his mouth.

"What the fuck is it now?" growled the lord of sin. "I was in the midst of practicing my swing."

He would have been better served hiring someone to dress him. "I need your help."

It was only then Lucifer noticed Marigold's shivering form. "What the fuck, Mictain? I thought you liked the girl."

"I didn't do this. Some of your demons did."

"Not under my orders," was the indignant reply.

"Renegades then. Doesn't matter. I've sent them to

dispatch for processing. But can we forget the who and how and get to the help part? She needs medical attention."

"So take her to a hospital."

"You know as well as I do that they're not equipped to deal with demonic poisonings."

"True. But she should have enough supernatural blood to help her pull through." She whimpered and Lucifer added, "Maybe."

"She's suffering."

"And? What do you want me to do about it? I'm a destroyer, not a fixer. If you wanted pansy healing magic you should have called Gaia."

"She's your girlfriend. You call her."

"Can't. She's on some spa day, girl's retreat thing with Muriel. No phones allowed. But she'll be back tomorrow."

Mictain's head just about exploded. "Then why tell me to call her if you knew she wasn't available?"

"I didn't. I was just saying that in this type of situation, should it ever happen again—"

"Alright. I get it. Can we move on? Time is a ticking."

"Fine. Be that way," Lucifer huffed. "Try to give some guy advice and he jumps all over you."

"Sorry. Happy now?"

"Not really."

"I'll buy you a grog next time we go out. Okay?" Because Lucifer was a cheap bastard who hated to pay for drinks. "Now, pop us back to my place, would you? I've got some stuff that should do the trick or at least alleviate the worst of her symptoms.

"I don't know. Maybe I should just take her straight to

her father. You haven't done too good of a job protecting her so far. Two demon attacks in two days? You're slipping, old man."

"Like hell. Who do you think saved her? As for taking Marigold to her dad, you heard her before. She's got no interest in the man."

"But she's injured now. That changes things."

"I can fix this. Don't get her father involved." Not when Marigold was at her weakest. She'd blow a gasket for sure when she recovered, and Mictain had enough apologizing to do as it was, starting with him not being around to protect her when she needed him most.

"If she dies…"

"Um, hello? Grim reaper here. I'll just refuse to collect her soul."

Lucifer snorted. "That's a dumb answer even for you. Good thing we're friends or I'd punish you for it. As for taking her back to your place, I'll give you both a ride, but don't say I didn't warn you."

What was the worst this so-called father could do?

The question took a back burner as the familiar rush of cold air followed by stifling hot and brimstone-tinged rushed past his face. In seconds, Lucifer had popped them to Hell, right into his bedroom. Mictain placed Marigold gently on the bed. How he wished he could have introduced her to his blue satin comforter under nicer circumstances.

Not liking her pallor at all, he ran to his bathroom and his first aid kit, which despite his assertion to Lucifer, proved disappointingly bare. Apparently, the shit had an expiration date. The potions for combating poison and increasing the rate of healing had dried out from disuse. Gods had little use for healing aids, and it seemed he'd owned his a tad too long.

"Fuck!" He raced back to his bedroom and checked on Marigold, who breathed shallowly. There was no help for it. He'd need to leave to get the medicine he needed. He kissed her lightly on the forehead. "Hold on, little witch. I'll be right back, and I promise you'll get better."

A part of him really didn't like leaving her alone, but there was no safer place for her than in his loft, which was only slightly less secure than Lucifer's personal quarters. Mictain did so prize his privacy.

Checking the wards first on his condo and finding them secure, Mick translocated himself right into Hell's apothecary, startling the hunched wizard-turned-pharmacist sitting behind the long, wooden counter.

"My lord, you do my shop great honor," said the wizened figure as he stood and bowed. "What may I help you with today? Perhaps a love agent to make the ladies swoon? We also have a new product sure to please; Hiagra two, the drug ensured to give you a monstrous cock, which unlike the first version, doesn't include the fangs."

Mictain restrained a shudder at the reminder of Hiagra 1. While he'd never tried it, the results of its use had horrified even the nastiest of denizens in Hell. "Thanks, Mungo, but what I really need is your strongest healing cream for a half-human and a counter agent to demonic poison."

"Hmm. I'll have to mix up a fresh batch. There's been an uncommon amount of demonic attacks lately." Mungo scurried to his lab in the back and Mictain paced, impatient at the wait even knowing it would take hours for the poison's effect to become irreversible. He couldn't help a nagging sense that something was wrong. *What a sap I'm turning into. She's safe at my place and I won't do her any good coming back without the medicine.*

Despite the alarm bells ringing madly in his mind, Mictain waited as Mungo carefully measured, stirred, and incanted. Finally, Mungo handed the two vials to Mictain, who with a terse "Thanks," popped back to his bedroom.

And an empty bed. *Are you fucking kidding me?*

"Lucifer!" Mick yelled his patron's name and didn't receive an answer. Not surprising given Mictain was sure he somehow had a hand in Marigold's disappearance.

Mictain popped himself so that he stood outside Lucifer's gate and rang the buzzer. No one, not even allies, could translocate directly into the compound. It was a pity no one had figured out how to prevent Satan from doing the same.

There was no answer to the buzzer, but the gate did swing open with an ominous creak. Lucifer carefully controlled the ambiance of his home and there was a strict rule against greasing the hinges on doors. Mictain strode up to the bronze front doors that stood close to twelve feet high. Lucifer received the strangest guests sometimes, and the features in his home, like oversized rooms and doors, were just a small indicator. The doors swung open with a metallic screech that made him wince.

Taking the gaping entranceway as an invitation, Mictain entered and strutted across the red slate floor directly to Lucifer's office. Satan's goblin secretary, her shiny green skin warted and her pointed teeth rouged for attention, just waved him through. As if she could have stopped him. Mictain wasn't in the mood to argue his lack of appointment, not with Marigold missing.

In he walked and found the Lord of Hades golfing; actually, he was putting, of a sorts. Lucifer held the leg of a demon as his club and appeared to be using the head as the ball, while the hole he aimed for was his pet hellhound who lay flat to the floor with its mouth wide open for its next treat. Familiar with the fate of others who interrupted—painful, and bloody—Mictain waited as Lucifer lined up his shot. Even silently cheered because he recognized the body parts as belonging to the fiends who'd attacked Marigold. What a way to go, dismembered, eaten, and then turned into hellhound shit. Satan had an eloquent sense of justice.

The foot at the end of the leg connected and the head rolled with an erratic wobble into the waiting maw. With a crunch, the dog devoured the head whole and Lucifer laid his makeshift club aside to pay him attention.

"Mictain, what a surprise," Lucifer said with a mocking smile.

"Where is she?" growled Mictain.

"Are you talking about the little witch? Yes, her father was most displeased with your lack of care. He decided she'd be better off with him after all."

"Get her back." Mick restrained an urge to shake Lucifer—one didn't lay hands on the Lord of Hades and expect to live to tell about it.

"Impossible."

"Then tell me where she is."

"Face it, Mictain, you've lost her. Now run along. I've

got a court session with a recently deceased BP executive. I want to make sure I'm in the proper mood." Lucifer rubbed his hands together with a sadistic smile.

Mictain exploded. "Dammit, Lucifer. She's my woman. If you know where she is, then tell me so I can at least try and talk to her father." Mictain hated feeling helpless. It wasn't something he'd encountered much in his life—or unlife. Despite knowing he should hold his temper, he couldn't rein it in, not with his emotions running so high. "I'm getting fucking tired of you meddling in my love life. It's none of your fucking business. Now tell me where the hell she is!"

It didn't take the smoke pouring from his ears for him to guess he'd gone too far. Lucifer turned to him with the fires of Hell snapping in his eyes. "Listen here, boy. I've tolerated your attitude because of our friendship, but you're really pushing it. Go home before you do something stupid. Forget the girl. She's out of your reach."

But Mictain wasn't about to forget Marigold. He couldn't; she'd gone and done the impossible. She'd stolen his heart. So, what was a god to do when he needed to find someone and the most powerful demon in the realm refused to help?

Mictain didn't bother saying goodbye. He just strode out of Satan's office and headed for the nearest open area where he could call upon his translocation magic. There was someone, make that a trio, who could possibly help him. The only problem was the price they might ask in return. Mictain didn't care. *I'll do or give anything.* He needed to find Marigold. Needed to make sure she was safe. Needed to hold her and never let her go.

Taking a deep breath, he popped to the top of Mount Purgatory. He landed on a barren plateau open on three sides. From the fourth side, carved into the mountain itself, gaped a cavernous opening. Welcome to the home of the Moirae, more commonly known as the Fates. The Moirae, like him, had lost all their followers as time marched on, but they still retained their powers. Although looking around him and where they'd chosen to live, Mictain wondered about their abilities. Unlike himself and other gods of ages lost to dust, the sisters did not seem to embrace modern times and its conveniences. He also had to wonder at their sanity at choosing to live in a dank cave dug into the very rock of Hades itself. Yet, doubt them as he might, he still needed their aid. He stood at the entrance to their home and called to them.

"Atropos, weaver of the beginning, I call upon you for aid." A warm breeze blew from the dark opening and swirled around his body, tickling him. "Lachesis, measurer of life, I call upon you for aid." Scent surrounded him—spicy, sweet, and sour—the various flavors a life should take. "Clotho, severer of life, I call upon you for aid." Deep cold came pouring forth, making his teeth chatter. The numbing chill of it sucked his breath away. Impressive tricks for a human; as a god, Mictain saw them for what they were—a sensory prop to make them seem more intimidating and mysterious.

Abruptly, all the sensations left him and, in a blink, before him stood three cloaked figures—Atropos in white for the purity of new life, Lachesis in a rainbow of colors for diversity, and black, of course, for Clotho, bringer of death. How cliché. Not that he said so. He did after all require their aid.

Keeping that in mind, he remained on his best behavior, calling upon the courtly manners he'd not used in millennia. Mictain bowed before the beings who had taken the shape of women for eons and hoped they had not read his earlier doubts, for this close to him, the power radiating from them was thick and unmistakable. *I'm surprised Lucifer hasn't tried to break them up. This kind of power all gathered in one place has to make him nervous.* Not his problem, though. He had more important things to worry about. "Fair ladies, thank you for granting me audience. You do me great honor," he said with a second deeper bow. With Satan, he had an open friendship that could stand the test of stress and harsh words, but with the Moirae, whose powers were vast, and their moods uncertain, he extended every courtesy.

"Speak your purpose." With their hoods drawn over their features and the voice, an eerie whisper, coming from all around him, he couldn't tell who'd spoken.

"I need helping finding a witch, a half-human named Marigold. She's been taken from me."

"Not taken so much as claimed by her father," a higher-pitched voice said with a titter.

"Taken," he asserted. "From my home and against her wishes."

"The rights of a father supersede those of a lover," countered a husky voice that crawled down his spine and made him shiver.

"He's not a father. She's never even met him. He abandoned her before her birth."

"And yet kept his eye upon her."

"And did nothing to protect her when she was attacked," he retorted.

"We see blood and mayhem should you choose to pursue her," the whispery voice warned.

Those words chilled him. "Who gets hurts? I don't give a damn about anyone else so long as I get Marigold back unharmed."

"From great need comes power. In the midst of battle, understanding dawns. By the blood shall arise that with the power to ream the world in two."

Mictain ran his hand through his hair, ruffling it. *Bloody Fates and their riddles.* "Okay, great. I'm sure that was a fabulous puzzle. But I'm not a bloody human, so I'd appreciate you dropping the act and just telling me where she is." He'd sort out the prophecy later and pray—to himself since he was after all a god—that the blood they spoke of wouldn't belong to Marigold.

"Find her you will, atop the mount."

"Mount what? Horse? Hilltop? Volcano? Could you be a little more specific?"

A loud sigh answered him. "Listen, our DVR's broken and we're missing our soap. Your girl's on mount Olympus. Is that clear enough? For payment, we are to be named honorary aunts for the children you will bear together. Now go away."

Say what? Before he could ask, the Fates disappeared in a swirl of smoke, and Mictain shouted, "Thank you" as the powdery mist floated back into the cave. Their words stunned him. *Children?* He hadn't thought that far ahead, but of course, if he continued to have sex with Marigold, the possibility existed. But he'd mull over that scenario later. He needed to prepare to storm the Olympian gods' playground. What fun! He couldn't remember the last time he'd launched or led an assault.

He'd require some help, though. Those Olympians tended to be violent, inbred snobs, which probably explained why Marigold's father—whichever god he was —had an issue with her taking up with him. A tanned Aztec wasn't exactly a toga-wearing buggerer.

Too fucking bad. Mick would wage a celestial war if forced so he could get Marigold back. *She's mine whether her daddy likes it or not. Time to call in my army. They could use the exercise.*

WARM SUNSHINE AWOKE MARIGOLD, the rays of bright light dancing across her skin. She opened her eyes to the view of a frescoed ceiling—a very disturbing one with beings engaged in perverted acts she was pretty sure weren't physically possible. She sat up only belatedly remembering her injuries. To her shock, she realized she felt fine. A quick glance down and pat of her body showed her healed and dressed in a short white robe.

"What the heck?" Last thing she remembered, she'd been on the losing end of a battle with demons. Then her lover arrived to the rescue. Was she in Mictain's home? She hopped out of bed and took stock of her surroundings. White walls, white bedding, and heavy, dark furniture. *And let's not forget the freaky artwork.* Somehow, the room didn't appear to be Mick's style, and yet, the last thing she remembered was him charging to her rescue.

Did I die? Had she in some really odd twist ended up in heaven? Nah. Even she wasn't dumb enough to believe a witch—and one who'd stolen her fair share of mascara as a teenager—would ever make it past the pearly gates.

But if I'm not up in the clouds then where am I? Spotting a window, Marigold strode over to the immense aperture flanked by sheer curtains that fluttered before a cool breeze. Her jaw dropped as she gaped at the view.

Fluffy clouds topped with gardens and palatial homes stretched before her. Despite her belief, it seemed the impossible happened. "How the hell did I end up in Heaven?" she exclaimed.

"Not Heaven, Mount Olympus, home of the Olympian gods," replied a deep voice from behind her.

Letting out a startled yelp, Marigold whirled and beheld an old man, tall of stature with craggy features partially hidden by his flowing white beard and hair. Forget tempering her language, not with her heart pounding in fright. "Who the hell are you?"

"I am Zeus, King of the Olympian gods, and your father."

If he expected his announcement to impress her, he was in for a surprise. "So you're the guy who knocked my mother up and abandoned her?" Marigold's voice came out even, surprising considering the rage boiling inside her. Finally, she'd found the object of her hate for so many years, and he stood—temptingly so—within reach of her wrath.

"Your mother was a mere mortal. You could not expect me to stay with her. I have duties," he announced with pomp.

"So why couldn't you bring her here?" Zeus didn't

recognize the flash in her eyes, the one that warned the storm was about to hit.

He looked incredulous. "What? You can't be serious? Bring my human lover here? My wife would have never stood for it."

Marigold lost it. "You were married! You pig. How dare you cheat on your wife? How dare you screw my mother over like that? Do you know she never got over you? Not only that, but she had to work like a dog just to keep a roof over our heads."

Zeus initially reeled under her accusations, but he quickly regrouped and his brows beetled together as he roared back," How dare you speak to me so disrespectfully? I am your father!"

"A deadbeat jerk is more like it," yelled Marigold, moving to stand toe-to-toe with him.

Zeus growled. "I will teach you to respect your elders."

"Get in line. Speaking of which, what did you do to Mictain?"

Zeus stepped back from her and smiled slyly. "Nothing, even though he deserved it for not protecting you. Nothing more than I'd expect from an Aztec dog."

"It's not his job to protect me. Now take me to him."

"No."

Marigold gazed upon the man who'd fathered her and wanted to scream with frustration. So much for her deeply buried fantasy of her father finding her and declaring he'd always loved and wanted her. She'd been right all along; her father was an ass. Mictain, however, wasn't, and Marigold wanted to see him something fierce. "Fine. Then I'll find him myself."

"You will do no such thing. You are my daughter and as such you will abstain from consorting with one of his ilk."

She gaped at him. "Excuse me? Did you just try to tell me who I may or may not date?" Marigold laughed. "Oh, that's freaking priceless. Let's get one thing straight, daddy dear," she said closing the space between them. "You *do not* tell me who I may or may not screw." She punctuated her words with hard pokes into Zeus's chest.

It amused her to see his face turn an interesting shade of purple. She expected a blistering reply, but instead, he turned and strode away. "I am the king of this domain. Your lover can't reach you here, and good luck trying to escape. You need to be a full Olympian god to navigate the treacherous path between here and the world below."

The door slammed on his way out and Marigold ran at it, yanking at the handle, which was, not surprisingly, locked.

She slapped the palms of her hands against the solid carved surface. "Let me out of here, you hairy has been." No answer. "Rotten, freaking jerk. See if you get a Hallmark card for Father's Day!" She kicked and pummeled at the hard panel to no avail. She whirled and eyed the room, looking for another exit. Spying the window, she sped across the room and looked out. The ground didn't look too far down. She could probably jump. She braced her hands on the sill and prepared to heave her legs over, only to hit an invisible barrier.

"You can't escape that way, dear."

She didn't scream as loudly this time, but the new intruder did somewhat startle her. Marigold whirled and found an attractive older woman standing in the room. She had brown hair touched with gray coiled atop her head and wore a long, beige gown cinched at the waist with a gold braided belt.

Great. Another Greek deity. "And who are you? My long lost sister?" asked Marigold sarcastically.

"Actually, given your parentage, I guess you could call me your step-mother. I'm Zeus's wife, Hera."

"Oh." Marigold lost her anger in a second and instead eyed the woman—a goddess if she remembered her mythology correctly—with wary eyes. "Hi."

Hera's face crinkled as she smiled. "Don't worry, child, I'm not angry at you for your father's transgressions, nor can I blame your mother. Mortals cannot resist the allure of a god."

"So you condone his cheating?"

"Of course not. Don't you worry, I've gotten my revenge for his philandering ways." The evil smile made Marigold grin in reply.

It also made her see a glimmer of hope. "So you don't agree with what he's done? Great, then you won't mind helping me escape."

"Why would I do that when your very handsome suitor has come to claim you?"

"What? Mictain is here?" Hope beat in her breast along with a warm, fuzzy feeling.

Hera swept a graceful hand toward the window, and Marigold turned around to look out. At first, she saw nothing, but a commotion in the distance finally caught her attention.

"See?" said Hera from beside her. "Your lover has come to free you from your father."

Marigold couldn't help the grin that stretched from ear to ear. *Mick came for me!* She lost her smile, though, when the sounds of clashing and yelling reached her ears.

"What's happening?"

"They battle to decide who shall win you, of course."

"But Mictain could get hurt." The thought appalled her. The stupid lug had come to mean a lot to her over the last few days. *I will kill him if he gets injured trying to rescue me.*

Hera held out her hand and a glowing light sparked into existence and grew until it resembled a hovering dinner platter. Its opaque surface cleared and Marigold beheld the battle as if she had a front row seat, replete with sound and smell—an added feature she could have done without because hordes of sweaty men did not exude a pleasant aroma.

But she forgot that, captivated by what she saw. Good god, and she meant that quite literally, was that Mictain swinging some odd thing that was a cross between a sword and club? Whatever it was, the weapon was deadly, and sliced with bloody efficiency.

But, a handheld weapon was no defense against a lightning bolt thrown at his back by her cowardly father.

Before he eyes, Mictain tumbled to the ground and didn't move. Marigold's heart stopped.

No.

Her lips moved silently as Zeus moved to stand over his motionless body, and she could see the deadly intent on his face.

Understanding his intent, rage bloomed to life within her, a molten inferno that needed release. "Like freaking hell!" With a scream of rage, Marigold blew a hole through the wall, her fury channeling power like she'd never imagined. Time to show daddy what she thought of his rules—and to rescue her lover.

14

MICTAIN CALLED HIS FORCES TOGETHER, other Aztec gods like himself, damned followers led by his general Montezuma, and he even had some demons in his ranks. Satan showed up as they began marching the perilous trail that led to Mount Olympus.

"Going somewhere?" asked Lucifer as he jogged along-side Mictain, who led the charge in full battle gear—loin cloth, war paint, and feathers.

"Just out for a run," said Mictain, lying smoothly.

"With an army?" puffed Satan, who gave up jogging to float effortlessly alongside. "I thought I told you to forget the girl."

"Who says this has anything to do with Marigold? I felt like starting a war and it occurred to me that the Olympians might be a good place to start."

Lucifer guffawed. "I knew you'd figure it out. So what's the plan? Kill her father and take her back?"

"Yup." He'd slaughter the whole lot of them to rescue her.

"You know she might have a problem with you killing her father even if she hates him right now."

"So I won't kill him. I'll just remove a body part or two."

Lucifer howled. "Oh, this is going to be fun. Mind if I tag along and watch?"

"Up to you, but I hope you're not wearing your good clothes, because I have a feeling things will get messy."

Lucifer sighed. "I wish I could play."

"Why don't you?" Mictain asked, curious at Lucifer's abstinence when he could clearly hear the longing to join in.

"Conflict of interest, or else I would. But if you ever decide to war against Heaven's army, let me know. I'll be there with bells on." Lucifer grinned wickedly and Mictain chuckled.

The path to Mount Olympus was treacherous—if the people approaching were human and idiots.

As a god, Mictain saw through the flimsy traps and led his army through without incident until they stood before the grand wrought iron gates—rather ostentatious if you asked him—leading into Olympus itself.

Mictain rapped his maquahuitl, a deadly, ancient Aztec weapon comparable to a sword but lined with enchanted obsidian, against the gates. "I am Mictain, Aztec god of death, and I come to claim my woman, Marigold, stolen from me by one of your cowardly denizens."

The air behind the gate swirled and a figure appeared. A tall, bearded man whom Mictain recognized as Zeus.

"Take your army, Aztec dog, and be gone," boomed Zeus with a fierce scowl.

"Not without my woman," replied Mictain. "My war is not with you, so tell her cowardly father to get his ass out here and deal with me himself."

"My daughter isn't going anywhere with you," replied Zeus with a smug smile. "So leave with your scraggly followers before I and my brethren show you what real gods are capable of."

Mictain smiled. His eyes lit with rage and his body warmed with a battle fever he hadn't enjoyed in a long time. "Then prepare for defeat." Mictain swung his maquahuitl and sliced through the bars blocking his way. "Death to the Olympians!" he screamed, leading the charge.

Mictain ran at Zeus, who'd jumped back from the fence, and swung low intending to lop off a leg instead of his head, just in case Marigold had changed her mind about her father. Zeus misted before his weapon could connect and reappeared a few hundred yards away, backed by the Olympian gods who appeared at his call.

Mictain's forces ranged out behind him, facing the aristocratic bunch that peered at them disdainfully. With a whooping cry, Mictain charged. His army, screaming wildly, followed him.

Their forces engaged with a mighty clash and noise that Mictain found invigorating despite the cause. His people, bloodlust roaring through their undead veins, jumped into the fray with little regard for their safety, unlike the Olympian gods who, while dressed pretty, seemed more concerned with staying clean than winning.

Battle lust giving him strength, Mictain swung his weapon with deadly accuracy, severing limbs left and right. None of his blows were fatal in the off chance his opponents were related to Marigold, but each well-aimed slice took his intended target out of the battle. It was obvious to Mictain before long that his forces were gaining the upper hand, but he'd forgotten one key thing about the Olympians.

Unlike his people, the Olympian gods had no honor. He only remembered this important fact as he felt the zinging zap from a bolt of electricity hit him in the back, flinging him to the ground, stunned.

Mictain blinked. He was far from dead, but he needed a moment for the force of the bolt to dissipate. His ears, however, were perfectly fine, and he clearly heard the scream—the cry of a severely pissed woman—that echoed around the battlefield.

That sounds like Marigold.

He no sooner thought that than he found himself flipped onto his back and staring up into the gloating visage of Zeus.

"Aztec dog. How dare you think to sully my daughter with your barbaric self?"

Mictain felt the tingle in his limbs indicating he was close to regaining full use of them. In the meantime, he smiled at Zeus through partially numb lips. "Marigold is mine. And when I'm done here, I'm going to take her home and claim her as my wife."

Zeus growled. "Not if I kill you first."

"Oh no you don't," spat Marigold, who arrived in a blur to stand over Mictain, which gave him an interesting view of what she wore under her white toga. Nothing at all. His cock hardened and Mictain's hands twitched as feeling came back to them. It occurred to him he should stand up and defend himself, but not only was the view much more interesting where he lay, he also wanted to see what Marigold would do next.

"Who let you out?" Zeus asked, not sounding the least bit happy about her escape.

"I let myself out, daddy dear," said Marigold in a sweet tone that screamed, to Mictain at least, how pissed she was.

"Impossible. Only a god could leave that room."

"Tell that to the hole in your wall. Now, I'm taking Mictain and his army and leaving. Do not try to stop me."

"Or what?" said Zeus, still cocky.

Mictain didn't see what she did, but he heard it. A swift thump followed by a groan. Mictain watched with a smirk as Zeus sank to his knees with watering eyes, his hands cupped to his abdomen.

"You hit me," Zeus accused. "You can't do that. I'm your father." Zeus ended on a whine that made Mictain wince. *Damned Olympians are so soft.*

"I warned you. And, if you want to be a father, how about starting with being nice to my boyfriend and not trying to lock me in rooms? Now, are you going to leave us alone, or am I going to have to demonstrate just how I blew that hole in the wall?"

"Fine. Leave. See if I care." Zeus pouted and Mictain almost felt sorry for the god. But not for long.

Marigold moved, and he lost the tantalizing view of

her bottom as she knelt beside him. Concerned eyes peered into his and her hands cupped his cheeks.

"Mick? Are you okay? Speak to me."

"A kiss," he whispered.

He'd no sooner spoken than her lips pressed against his, sweet and soft. Desire ignited throughout him and his body, free of the electrical zap, sprang to life—well, his cock did anyway. Mictain brought his arms up and dragged her on top of him. She gasped. He grinned and rolled her under him in one swift motion.

He kissed her as his body pressed into her. He couldn't even describe how happy he was to see her. His cock knew how it wanted to show her. He just needed to rid them of the material between them so it could demonstrate and sink himself into her body. He needed...

A throat cleared. "I dare say, while I for one am quite into watching as the two of you get it on, don't you think that you should release your army first so they can get some action of their own?"

Mictain groaned and rolled off Marigold. He really didn't want to. She looked so beautiful with her cheeks flushed and her eyes bright with passion. She didn't make things easier when she gave him a sultry smile.

"Hold that thought," he told her as he turned to face his troops who stood grinning over the downed and cowering Olympians. Mictain smiled back. *People might foolishly think Aztecs are barbarians, but when it comes to battle, we kick ass.*

Mictain opened his mouth to thank them and order them home when Marigold spoke first. "Brave warriors, thank you for coming to the aid of my lover, the god of death himself, Mictain. Your bravery will not be forgotten. And as a thank you for participation in my rescue, free drinks at—" Marigold paused.

"Montezuma's Revenge," supplied Mictain.

"Courtesy of my newly found father." Zeus grumbled and Marigold hissed at him. "Shut up and consider it a small price and a start in your path to my forgiveness." Marigold turned to Mictain and pressed herself against his front. "Now, what's a girl need to do to get a certain god naked and in a shower with her?"

Mictain threw Lucifer a glance.

Satan sighed. "Again? The things I do for my friends." A snap of his fingers and they were in Mictain's bathroom —army, Lucifer, and meddling father free.

Alone. Thank fuck.

Marigold faced him with a smile and reached for the tie at her shoulder to remove the toga, but Mictain stopped her. "Leave it on and turn around," he asked, his voice thick. He could still clearly see her sweet pussy as she'd straddled him on the battlefield, and he needed it, *now*.

Marigold turned and braced her hands on the wall. She peered at him over her shoulder and gave him a coy smile as she wiggled her butt.

"Tease!" With a growl, he flipped up the skirt of her toga. He slid a hand between her cheeks and ran it across her wet slit. He loved how she was so ready for him without even a touch.

"Don't tease me," she asked, her voice low and sensual.

He needed no further invitation. He dropped his loin cloth, letting his cock spring forward. He slapped it off her ass cheeks, teasing her, a game he lost when she bent right over and exposed herself to him. No sane man, or god, could have resisted.

He drove his shaft into her, promising to make up for his haste later, too enflamed to wait a moment longer. He needed to feel her clenched tight around him. But he wasn't the only one primed and ready. Slick and molten, her pussy took every inch of him and she mewled for more. He dug his fingers into her ass cheeks and pounded her willing flesh. Faster he plowed, urged on by her excited cries. He also couldn't resist slapping her fleshy ass. His hand connected and she cried out as her pelvic muscles tightened around his thrusting cock. Mictain shouted at the exquisite sensation.

"Again," she panted.

The smack of his hand hitting her pale flesh made her squeeze tight once again and with a bellow, Mictain couldn't hold back. He came, his final thrust thankfully triggering her climax.

He waited only a moment for her tremors to subside before straightening and turning her into his arms. He didn't give her a chance to speak. His lips claimed hers in a fiery kiss as his hands divested her of her clothing. Her hands were equally busy, removing the feathers decorating him, and within moments, they were both naked and standing in the hot spray of his shower.

He tried to wash her and she him, their hands stroking and soaping. Yet, even with the quickie against the wall, Mictain was still impatient. The feel of her hot, slick flesh against his drove him wild, and his cock hardened again. His urgency seemed an equal match to hers judging by the way her hands roamed up and down his body while her mouth clung to his with panting need.

He dropped to his knees in the shower, nuzzling her pubes. She grabbed at his wet hair and gazed down on him, her eyes heavy with desire. "Lick me," she ordered.

He needed no further urging. He spread her legs and with his hands holding her up, he buried his face into the apex of her thighs. She whimpered and clung to him as he tortured her sensitive clit, his tongue flicking the engorged nub.

"Lean against the wall," he said gruffly. When she complied, he kept one hand on her to hold her up, but used the other to delve between her plump lips. He groaned at the tight feel of her squeezing around his digits. He finger fucked her, his index finding and stroking her g-spot. She quivered at his touch, her honey running down his hand. He found her clit again with his tongue as he stroked her, frantically working her until, with a scream, she came, her sex clamping around his fingers. But he wasn't done yet.

He stood and palmed her rounded ass cheeks. He squeezed them before lifting her up until her slick core was aligned with his cock. With a grunt, he pushed into her eager sex, still trembling from its climax. Her flesh sucked him in and her legs wrapped around his flanks, locking him in tight. Mictain groaned.

"Oh yes," she murmured, burrowing her face against his neck.

Leaning her against the tile wall of the shower, he started slow, his thick shaft slipping in and out her tight sheathe, but her excited cries and nails digging into his shoulders soon had him increasing his pace. Faster he pumped her until she screamed his name and came, her flesh quivering around him in constricting waves that had him shuddering and climaxing hard inside her.

When the tremors in their bodies subsided, he let her slide down his body. He turned her until she stood under the hot spray of the shower. She leaned back into him and he hugged her to his chest.

"Thanks for coming to save me," she said softly.

"Always. I'm sorry your dad turned out to be such a disappointment."

Marigold turned in his arms and looked up at him. "Bah, I expected that. What I didn't expect was an Aztec god gathering an army and declaring war for me."

Mictain grinned. "Turns out you didn't need my help, but at least my men got some exercise."

Marigold returned his smile. "Hey, does this mean I'm a demi-god then?"

"In my eyes, you are definitely a goddess." She blushed and dropped her gaze. Mictain held back a chuckle. Brazen she might be, but she melted at compliments, something he'd have to remember. "Stand still now while I wash you. I need a clean canvas for the dirty things I intend to do to you later."

"I'll hold you to that," she teased

Mictain grabbed the bar of soap and cleaned her, kneeling to wash even the soles of her feet. She giggled and he looked up at her.

"That tickles," she said with a shrug and a smile.

She looked so adorable. The words burst from him before he could stop them. "I love you."

———

Marigold froze for a second, not out of fear or an urge to run, but because he'd stunned her, in a good way. She also realized in that instant something very important, quick and impossible as it seemed. "I love you too."

He stood, his face brimming with happiness, and his arms curled around her possessively. "Mine," he claimed, hugging her tight.

"Yours," she agreed. "And you are mine as well, forever."

"Forever indeed," he agreed.

"Wow, that's a long time to commit to considering your life span," said Satan's mocking tone from outside the shower.

"Lucifer!" bellowed Mictain while maneuvering Marigold behind him.

Marigold laughed and wrapped her arms around Mictain's body from behind. As he argued with the Lord of Hades about boundaries and ground rules, Marigold reflected on her good fortune.

Who'd have thought a date with death would end up with me falling in love with a god, and not just any god, but the hottest and nicest god ever. This is one case where death can take me whenever he likes—naked, of course.

EPILOGUE

"Um, Mick honey, could you come here please?" Marigold blocked Satan's way into their home, having foiled his impromptu indoor visits by placing a powerful spell on Mick's loft, their home in Hell.

The Lord of Hades tried a puppy dog look that made her bite her lip so she wouldn't giggle. "Ah, come on, Marigold. Just let me in. I got to talk to Mick."

"Let him in, Mari." Mick arrived and pulled her away from the door into the comfort of his body. She never tired of him touching her. Several weeks into their new life together and she was happier than she ever remembered being.

"What do you want, Lucifer?" she asked, having a sneaky suspicion already.

"Listen, Zeus is really sorry about everything that's happened. He really wants to make it up to you."

"I'm sure he does," she said. "But until he's ready to apologize to Mick, I have no interest in talking to him."

"That's just it. He's given in to your demands," Satan announced triumphantly.

Marigold's brow furrowed. "I don't get it. What suddenly made him change his mind?"

Satan grinned devilishly. "Why, the baby, of course. He couldn't very well hate the father of his grandchild now, could he?"

Marigold gaped at Satan and Mick's hold around her tightened as he whispered in her ear. "Well that would certainly explain your bigger boobs."

Marigold turned to give him a quick glare before turning back to Lucifer. "What makes you all think I'm pregnant? Don't you think I would have noticed?"

"The Moirae came over for tea yesterday and were quite giddy over the fact they are about to become aunts. I have to say, I'm a little hurt no one asked me to be an uncle. It's a good thing I'm not easily offended."

Marigold laughed at the not so subtle hint. "Fine, you can be an uncle, but please leave the corrupting to us."

Lucifer rubbed his hands with glee. "Great. So can I tell Zeus all is forgiven?"

"Tell him he can come for dinner and to bring Hera. But you warn him, one nasty word and he's out on his ear."

"No problem. Hera will make him behave. See you at the baby shower." Satan went to pop out only to grunt in annoyance. "Stupid shielding spell." He stalked over to the front door and let himself out.

Seconds later, Marigold was whirling in circles held aloft by Mick. "A baby. Our baby," he crowed.

She grinned at his enthusiasm. Life was about to get

more interesting, and to think, she had her freckles to thank for it. "I love you, Mick."

The spinning stopped, and Mick turned serious. "I love you too, Marigold. Thanks for almost dying."

"Anytime for you," she teased. "Just think of what an awesome story it's going to make to tell our child."

With those words, she was spinning again, but giddy with love and happiness, she laughed. *Who'd have guessed when Death came calling, I'd not only get naked and invite him into bed, but also let him stake a place in my heart.*

———

WHISTLING, LUCIFER POPPED BACK INTO HIS PALACE. GAIA peeked up from the wilted plant on his desk. "What's got you so giddy?"

"I am not giddy, woman. Merely pleased at another perfectly executed plan."

"Perfect? You caused a war."

"Bah. They needed some excitement in their lives. Look at the end result. Another happy couple. A baby on the way, and Zeus in my debt for reconciling him with his daughter."

"Only you would see yourself as the hero in all this."

"Ugh. You're right. Think it's too late to claim the spot of villain?"

"It's never too late for you to get evil."

"I say we celebrate with some hot and sweaty sinning." He leered and waggled his brows suggestively.

She hiked her frothy green skirt and ran with a taunting laugh.

He chased.

And when he caught her, the resulting tsunami raised the isle of Atlantis. But that's a story for another day.

The End (of this story)

But the fun continues…A Demon and her Scot

Milton Keynes UK
Ingram Content Group UK Ltd.
UKHW040846050124
435493UK00005B/568

9 781988 328737